ANCHOR POINT

THE INLAND SEAS SERIES - BOOK 4

GWYN MCNAMEE

Anchor Point
by Gwyn McNamee © 2020

Cover Design: Michelle Johnson at Blue Sky Designs
Cover Models: Chris Hayman and Desiree Lyn
Photographer: Wander Aguiar
Editing: Wallflower Edits

To realize the worth of the anchor, we need to feel the stress of the storm.

Corrie ten Boom

ACKNOWLEDGMENTS

Anchor Point was an emotional book to write. I can't thank the people who helped me with this book. Christy, Renee, and Stephanie, you guys ROCK! And, as always, I owe a huge thank you to my husband for always supporting my work and making sure I have time at the computer so get things done.

1

ELIJAH

The freezing spray coming up over the bow of the *Calista* batters my skin, but it does nothing to quell the boiling hot rage surging through my blood. Even the bitterest February cold out on the lake can't do anything about that.

I can't believe I'm back here again. After all this time. After all these years.

My hands clench around the rail, and I close my eyes and let the brutal winter weather on Lake Michigan attack every exposed inch of my body. My bare arms and face take the brunt of it, burning and stinging with the brutal force of Mother Nature. I stand here and take it all, but no amount of self-flagellation will absolve me of my sins. The ones that brought me here, to where I am today, about to face my greatest enemy...again.

There's no way I should be here. And everyone knows it.

I shake my head and suck in a cleansing breath of the biting cold air. I should've stayed back at the warehouse. I should've told them *no*.

The moment Valentina mentioned the Albanians, I

should've shoved away from that table and told them all to *fuck off*.

But I didn't.

I sat there in stunned silence while she asked us to raid yet another ship of one of her rivals—one I know all too well.

Her request wasn't a surprise. She always has us going after some sort of shipment from her competitors. And I would love to let myself believe it's with altruistic intent, but we all know what's happening. She's the head of one of the most powerful criminal organizations in the Midwest, and she wants her rivals gone, their supply chains and resources interrupted.

I can't say I blame her. She's trying to maintain control over a territory in flux. One being attacked from all sides by the cartels, by the Albanians, by the Irish and Russians, by every goddamn organization in Chicago.

It should give me comfort to know what we're about to do today is going to help fuck up the lives of the people who ruined mine, but it doesn't. It can't. Nothing can temper the ache in my heart or the scorching burn in my soul—the anguish I live with every fucking day because of my choices and because of *them*.

I force open my eyes and glance behind me to the wheelhouse. Cutter stares back at me from behind the wheel. Or should I say, stares back at me from behind the shades. Even with me, he can't take them off. Valentina is the only one who's managed to break that down, and only when she's alone with him. Around us, the men who have been his brothers for so long, he's still the same closed-off asshole as always.

He motions for me to return inside. I probably should before I fucking freeze to death. Though, maybe that's what I really want deep down. To die an agonizing death.

Maybe it's what I deserve.

Though death would be too easy. A simple way out to end my suffering. Life would never give that to me. Enduring this agony day in and day out is the only way to pay, the only *fair* consequence.

I take another deep breath before I shove away from the rail and stumble across the slippery, wet deck to the door. I heave it open and step into the warmth of the small room. A shiver rolls through me, and I shake off the water clinging to my skin and run a damp hand over my wet face and through my soaked hair. Goose bumps break out all over my body, and my limbs start to shake—though whether it's a potential early sign of hypothermia or my nerves is a toss-up. I grab a towel hanging next to the door and wipe my face, even though we're just going to get wet again in a few minutes.

"We're almost there." Cutter's announcement only confirms what I already know.

It was almost like I could sense it looming in the distance, even though we weren't close enough for me to see it when I was out there.

I focus on the front window and the water beyond it. Through the sleet and spray at the bow, I can just make out the ship.

The ghost ship. The *Wanderer.*

She shouldn't even be here. Not this time of year. February in the lakes is usually controlled by thick ice on the water that ships can only move through at a snail's pace with an ice-breaking barge in front of them, or they don't move on the water at all.

The lakes are practically shut down from December to March, and sometimes even longer, depending on how the weather turns. That's why this ship got Valentina's attention. It showed up at the Soo Locks when there hadn't been a ship through there for weeks. This ship is taking advantage of the unusually warm temperatures and the ice break up.

And Valentina has been watching for it.

She has spies in every camp in Chicago, it seems. People

unscrupulous enough to sell her information and rat out their own organizations. I don't know if she knows what's on the ship or not. All that matters is she wants to have it and them not to.

Would it have changed things if I had told her no? That I wouldn't do it?

Probably not.

It only would have made the job harder for the rest of the crew to take down the ship one man down.

Though my being here may not help them much. My head isn't in the right place to be doing this. And they all recognize it.

Cutter's attention flicks over to me before returning to what's in front of us. "Are you sure you're okay? You can stay on the boat. You don't have to—"

I hold a hand up to stop him. "I'm fine."

It's a fucking lie, and he knows it.

But Cutter is the one who isn't going to press me. If anyone would, it would be Rion or Preacher. They won't, though. Not today. Not with this. Both of them learned very early on after I joined the crew that it wasn't something I was going to talk about, and what we're doing now doesn't change that.

They don't need to know all the details. And I don't need to relive them. I already do that enough in my head every fucking day of my life.

I flip open the bench in the wheelhouse and pull out our rifles. After a quick once-over to make sure they're loaded, I grab a couple of extra magazines for my Glock. "You loaded up?"

Cutter nods and lifts his shirt, showing me his pistol and ammo.

I leave the guns on the top of the bench and watch our approach to the *Wanderer*. The *Destiny* rolls in the water alongside our target.

We couldn't play this like we normally do. The whole distressed pleasure craft game doesn't really work in the middle of Lake Michigan in February. Just like this cargo ship shouldn't be here, no one should be out this far, either, especially on a yacht.

Our only choice was to use the *Destiny* as the decoy. A fishing vessel is the only thing that might not draw too much attention or unwanted questions. But even with her here to get the *Wanderer* to stop, we have to go in hard and fast. There's no room for error. They're going to know exactly what our purpose is.

It's not ideal, but Valentina swears it's necessary to take whatever is on this ship. One thing I learned about that woman over the last six months is that she doesn't do anything just because. She's wicked smart and knows her business. *Il Padrone* taught her well in the short time she was with him. And I trust her. Especially after what she did for Everly. If her source told her something important is coming in, then it's our job to ensure it doesn't reach Chicago.

Even at a great personal cost to myself.

We bounce over the choppy waves churned up by the winter winds, and I grab one of the ARs and tighten my hand around it. We're as prepared as we can be. This is what we do. Yet, the nerves that are usually absent during our missions won't dissipate. Just knowing who the men on that ship work for has me wound so tightly, I might snap.

The radio crackles to life. "We're ready." Warwick's deep voice booms over the static. "No contact with them since they stopped."

"Roger that." Cutter's brief reply is all that's needed.

This mission has been planned out down to every last detail, just like they always are before we even set foot on these ships. Before we even agree to do it.

The only problem is the unknown.

When they came through the locks, the information indicated six crewmen. But for such a big ship, that seems like a small crew. My guess is they may have paid someone off to avoid a closer inspection. Not unheard of and actually quite the norm up there. Especially this time of year, it would be easy to slip through with whatever cargo you wanted, basically untracked.

That doesn't bode well for us. But this isn't the first time we've been in this situation. We know what to do even if we face something we're not expecting.

The ship looms ominously over us, and we draw closer. No movement or response from the crew aboard the *Wanderer,* even though they must have seen us coming. We pull behind the *Destiny*, but no gunfire greets us yet.

Why aren't they firing?

Unease crawls through me. They're getting ready for a fight. It's the only explanation.

We tie up to the ship, and Cutter eyes me one last time as he tosses his shades onto the counter in the wheelhouse and replaces them with his NODS goggles that give us such a huge advantage in a firefight. "You're sure?"

"Fuck you, man." I blow past him and push out the door onto the slick deck.

He follows on swift feet and shoves me out of the way to ascend the ladder first. His place is at the head of the pack, and he's not about to let me charge in first. Not when he doesn't trust me to keep my shit together today. Warwick and Rion climb onto our bow from the back of the *Destiny* to board with us.

Again, it's not ideal. We'll be sitting fucking ducks coming up on one single ladder, but the ship doesn't offer any other entry points, probably by design.

What the fuck do they have below deck?

It's something major enough to get Valentina's attention.

Drugs? Guns? Other weapons to help them wage war in Chicago?

Whatever it is, it's not getting to them. Not if we have anything to say about it.

We follow Cutter up, one by one, with Rion bringing up the rear. When Cutter reaches the top, he pauses and peeks over the rail. I try to glance up to scan the deck, but from this position, all I see is the metal side of the boat...and Cutter's ass.

He pulls up his rifle, holds out his hand for a second to tell us to wait, then climbs over the rail. Gunfire erupts almost immediately from his left, and he returns fire, providing me cover as I leap over the rail after him.

The bullets whiz past me, pinging off the metal bulkheads and rails around me, and a sharp pain strikes my left arm.

Fuck.

I return fire and dive behind a stack of crates on the deck. Cutter's right next to me, and he fires around the edge of the crate as Warwick and Rion race our way.

They dive for cover with us, and Rion eyes my arm. "You all right?"

"Just a graze. I'm fine."

It's nothing compared to the one I took the first time I was shot or the one that hit me in the leg on the *Marcella Marie*. That hurt like a fucking bitch, and if it had been an inch over, I would've bled to death in seconds. This is just a flesh wound. Nothing more than a scratch really. The blood isn't even dripping to the deck.

Cutter peers around the crates and fires again. "I took out two on the way over here. One more just now. Do you guys see anybody else?"

I shake my head. "No, but there has to be somebody in the wheelhouse."

He nods his agreement. "And probably someone below deck with the cargo." He motions backward toward the wheelhouse. "Rion and War take the wheelhouse. E and I will go below."

Warwick peeks around the other side of the box. "We'll go this way. I see the door for the staircase to the wheelhouse." He motions for Rion to follow him, and they creep to the edge of the crate and disappear around the side.

I shove to my feet, and Cutter and I move in the opposite direction, directly for the door that leads down to the cargo bays, using the row of crates as cover.

Cutter nudges the ajar metal door, and it creaks open to a dim, descending staircase. He motions down, and I follow him into the darkness. With those goggles, he can see everything. I should be wearing mine, too—something Cutter would have insisted on under other circumstances—but I haven't been thinking clearly since hearing the word "Albanians" a week ago.

Every moment since then has been a mix of vivid, blood-red memories and hazy ones I try to push deeper into my psyche. No wonder Cutter wonders if I'm okay. I'm clearly not.

But I can't let it break my concentration right now. It could cost one of us our lives.

We reach the bottom of the stairs, and Cutter pulls a bullet from one of his magazines and tosses it out into the room in front of us. It draws fire from the far-right side of the cavernous space.

At least we know where some of the crew are, but they could be scattered all over the cargo area.

"There's only one." The soft, accented voice comes from our right, so faint, I'm barely sure I heard it.

I squeeze Cutter's shoulder. He nods. He heard it, too.

Who the hell else is down here? And can we trust what we just heard?

If there is only one, we know exactly where he is, but the other possibility—that we're being set up to walk into a blood bath—is also very likely.

Cutter quickly peeks around the edge of the stairwell. He

leans back to me and indicates he has eyes on one crewmember. He's going to eliminate him. Even with his limited vision, he's still a crack-shot. He crouches down and shifts the barrel of his AR around the corner.

A single shot is all it takes.

Cutter rises and motions for me to follow him. We need to do a sweep of the cargo bay—to make sure we got every crewmember and to figure out who the fuck whispered that information to us.

He steps around the corner and freezes. "Holy shit."

"What?"

He shoves me back behind him to the safety of the wall of the stairwell. "There are heat signatures everywhere down here. Dozens of them."

"Then why aren't they firing at us?"

Even in the dim evening light streaming down the stairs from the deck, I can see his lip twist up into a sneer.

"I don't know. Maybe they aren't crew. The one I took out had a rifle and was standing. These are all lower, on the floor."

"None of us are armed. You're safe." The same gentle voice floats across the cargo bay, louder this time. "Turn on the light. There's a switch on the wall to your right."

What the fuck is going on?

Cutter gestures to the right, and I reach over and fumble 'til my hand finds the switch. He lifts the NODS from his face, and I flip it on. We both blink against the florescent overhead lights, then step cautiously around the corner, our guns raised and ready for anything that might be waiting.

"Holy shit..." The rest of the words die on my lips.

"Jesus fucking Christ."

That about sums it up.

My eyes take in the scene in front of me, but my mind can't seem to grasp what I'm seeing.

Women.

Dozens and dozens of them.

Huddled together in corners.

Bound with ropes or handcuffs at their ankles and wrists.

Shivering.

Dirty.

Half-naked.

Christ...they're smuggling women.

Bile climbs up my throat, and I swallow it back and spin to survey what's before me. The rifle in my hand shakes, and a cold sweat breaks out over my skin.

How could anyone do this?

Cutter turns to the left and wanders down the rows toward the body of the crewmember he shot. Women cower away from him and whisper things to each other. I can't say I blame them.

What these women must have been through already...

I shake my head to dispel the disgusting visions of every horrible possibility and twist toward where the mysterious voice came from when we were still in the dark.

Cutter would have eventually gotten the guy on his own, but the whispered words still assisted in what could have turned into a bloody firefight where some of these innocent women might have been hurt in the crossfire.

A pair of small, dirty feet protrude from a dark corner to my right. I approach slowly, my finger shifting closer to the trigger, just in case this is some sort of trap. The feet disappear into the shadows. The cowering form tucked against the wall is barely visible.

I point my AR into the darkness and flip on the TAC light mounted on the scope. A petite, dark-haired woman holds up bound hands to block the stream of light from falling on her face. Heavy chains wind around her wrists, twist across her chest and stomach, and encircle her small ankles.

A dirty dress barely covers her tiny frame and can't conceal the bruises on her tanned skin.

She isn't a threat. She's a damn prisoner.

I slowly lower my weapon to take the light from her face. Her hands gradually drop. A pair of wide, frightened hazel eyes stare back at me from under thick, dark lashes. Her entire minuscule frame vibrates, rattling the chains around her.

She's fucking terrified. And why wouldn't she be?

These men probably snatched her from a street somewhere. I don't even want to *think* about what they might have done to her between then and when we stormed this ship. And now, a big, tattooed man with a gun is standing over her, and she just saw Cutter kill the crewmember with a single shot.

She doesn't know who we are or our intent. I'm sure the only reason she helped us was in hopes that we would be the lesser of two evils compared to her captors. We could be the buyers coming out here to collect these women and take them to their final fates. She has no reason to trust that we won't hurt her...or worse.

I squat down slowly and hold up my hands. "Are you the one who told us where he was?" I motion over my shoulder toward the opposite corner of the vast space where Cutter stands with the body.

She swallows thickly and nods. "Yes."

The single word is barely a whisper. If I weren't right in front of her, I wouldn't have even heard it.

"Why did you help us?"

Her eyes narrow in on my gun, her fear darkening them. "Because I was hoping you were here to rescue us."

My heart sinks into my stomach.

We're not rescuers. Not at all.

Valentina sent us here for the cargo, to disrupt whatever plans the Albanians had. There's no way she knew these fuckers were trafficking women. If she had known, she would have warned us. She never would have sent us out here completely unprepared to do anything to help these women.

All we can do now is leave and hope it doesn't take too long for the Coast Guard to find the ship. But considering the time of year and the fact that the ship shouldn't even be here, that could be a long fucking time they're stuck down in this hold, shivering and petrified for their damn lives.

Just like she probably was...

I shake my head and clench my eyes shut.

No. I can't go there.

Not now.

"E!"

I blink away the anguish threatening to unravel me and rise to turn and face Cutter. He closes the distance between us and spares a passing glance at the woman in the corner.

He motions for me to follow him back to the staircase, then leans into me. "We need to let Warwick and Rion know what's down here."

I nod my agreement and scan the room again. "What can we do?"

He blows out a long breath and sighs. "Not much. Maybe once we're back at the warehouse, Preacher can somehow alert the Coast Guard, so they aren't sitting out here too long."

It will still be almost half a day before we make it home. Nothing moves fast on the lake, especially this time of year.

We can't just leave them like this.

Cutter's hand closes around my bicep. "I know what you're thinking, but they can't be our problem. They aren't our responsibility, E. We need to cover our own asses and make sure we get away clean. I policed our brass down here and will get the stuff on the deck, and then there's nothing else that can lead to us. I'll go tell War what's going on." He glances back at the women in the room. "Keep an eye on them."

What the hell else am I supposed to do?

2

EVANGELINE

The man with the horrific scars covering half his face disappears up the stairwell. A tiny bit of relief hits me. That man is a stone-cold executioner. There's no doubt about that. He took out that crewmember in a split-second. A single shot. But the other one...he carries himself differently. He glances back at me from where he stands at the bottom of the stairs.

It's there in his blue eyes before he turns away again. The pity. The knowledge of what's happened to all of us. The fact that he and the men he came with have no intention of helping us. They're going to leave us here—wherever we are—with no food. No water. No medical care. They're going to leave our fates in someone else's hands. They aren't here for us.

I knew it the moment the lights came on and I saw they weren't in police or military uniforms. This isn't the Coast Guard. This isn't some military force sent to help trafficking victims.

No. Not even close.

These men are criminals. Killers. They're no better than the ones who snatched me off the street and took me away from the life I knew.

These men are just as dangerous as the ones who chained me to this wall. The ones who tortured all of us and intended to sell us to the highest bidders when we got to our destination.

I have to remember that...no matter what happens.

They are the enemy, too.

Several of the women in the room begin to stir and sit up or rise to their feet, if their restraints allow it. Our captors always made sure the ones who caused problems were securely tied with no room for movement. Excited chatter fills the air in a dozen different languages—only a few of which are familiar.

There are other Filipino girls here, others like me who were taken by those monsters and handed over to the Albanians or other traffickers in the open ocean off the islands. And there are others from different places who have been picked up along the way. Still others have been part of this life—if you can call it that—for years. Women who are simply traded between different monsters. Some of them have been in this Hell since they were mere children. They've never known a loving home, or they had one so long ago they don't even remember it.

Maybe that would be preferable. To have no memory of a real life. No recollection of the people and places they called home. The warm, loving arms that once held them and protected them. Maybe that makes it easier to be here like this, or maybe they are just better at coping with it after all this time. They've accepted their fates and are simply making the best of it while those of us still new to the horror weep and fight back against an enemy we can't beat.

Tears blur my vision, and I swipe them away with the back of my hand. The movement zaps the little energy I have left. I've cried enough for ten lifetimes in the weeks I've been on the ship. Or maybe it's been months? Any sense of time disappeared long ago. And what does it matter anyway?

I cried for Ma. I cried for Pa. I cried for the life I will never be able to go back to.

And that knowledge—the absolute confidence that my past life is gone forever—is what gives me the strength to clear my bone-dry throat and force out the words. "Take me with you."

The man with the sandy-blond hair and piercing Caribbean eyes whirls around to face me. A muscle tics in his jaw, and he takes several steps toward me, scanning the women around us. "What did you say?"

Louder. Make sure he understands.

There can be no doubt what I want. What I *need* from him. If I leave room for doubt, it may be what kills me.

"Take me with you." I try to tug at the chains, try to get closer to him so he can hear me above the excited chatter of the women and other sounds of the ship. But I can't move. Exhaustion, the fever that's been raging through my body for days, and the heavy chains wrapped around me weigh me down.

I sag against the restraints, and my eyes drift closed, the effort it takes to keep them open far too much for me to muster. The metal at my wrists bites into my raw skin, but I'm too tired to cry out from the pain. Too damn tired to do anything but make one final plea to this stranger for help.

The corners of his mouth droop into a frown, and he squats in front of me, putting himself at my level. "I can't do that. And you wouldn't want to come with me anyway, sweetheart."

"Anywhere is better than here." My words sound desperate because they are. I won't survive if he leaves me. I won't last, mentally or physically. The darkness has been creeping in around the edges of my vision for days, threatening to take me. And I haven't been fighting it. It's a welcome relief from the terror of my world. Yet, I've kept breathing somehow. Kept suffering.

This is my only chance.

He sighs and runs a hand through his hair as he drops his

head back to stare at the ceiling. A silent moment passes, where it seems the entire cargo hold vanishes and it's only the two of us. Him fighting with a decision. Me waiting to learn my fate.

When his eyes meet mine again, the compassion there shreds what's left of my eviscerated soul. "No, you don't. It's not. It might take a little while, but the Coast Guard will find you. They'll take you somewhere safe until every one of you can be sent back home. Wherever home is."

An errant tear rolls down my cheek despite my best efforts to suppress them. If I panic, if I come across as crazed, he won't take what I have to say seriously. He won't understand how important this is. "The Philippines, for me, at least. Other places for some of the women. But...I can't go back there."

His brow furrows, and he shifts his weight, resting his gun across his knees. "What do you mean you can't go back? Don't you have family there? A life?"

I swallow through the lump in my throat and shake my head. The motion sends the room spinning, and I have to close my eyes, so I don't pass out. "Not anymore. I can't go back."

He doesn't understand. He can't. But I need him to.

The man who holds my freedom in his hands pushes to his feet and studies the wall above my head instead of meeting my gaze. "I'm sorry. I can't. But you'll be okay. I promise you that."

He turns on his heel and strides to the other side of the cargo hold without a glance in my direction.

Heartless bastard.

But I don't know what I expected.

Why would he help me? Why would he take a woman like me with him?

I shiver and rest my temple against the cold metal of the wall that keeps me chained in this godforsaken place. This wall has been my home for so long, it's almost comforting.

Icy steel against my hot skin. Solid and hard against my weak and broken body.

It keeps me upright when all I want to do is sag onto the floor and let the blackness engulf me.

Footsteps echo down the stairs, and his friend reappears. They meet across the room and bow their heads together in a heated discussion. The man with the scars jerks his head and looks toward me, then returns to his friend and plants a firm hand against his chest. Something is said, too low for me to make out.

The kind man must have told the scarred one what I said. What I asked for. And he doesn't look very happy about it.

I need them to understand. I can't go back.

They move back toward the stairs.

They're going to leave me.

"Wait." My shout reverberates through the vast space, and all the women stuck here with me turn and gape in my direction. They want out just as badly as I do, but many are probably desperate to get home to their families, to their loved ones, to the people who will care for them and protect them and get them back to regular life. That's something I can never have again.

"Please wait." These words are nothing more than a whisper. I'm fading fast. There isn't much time.

The weight of my eyelids is more than I can handle. My eyes droop closed, and another shiver wracks my body. The fever that's been ravaging my body for the last few days has taken its toll. I try to shift against the wall, to pull myself up, but I crumble and let the tears fall.

Something shuffles in front of me. Boots clank on the metal floor. I manage to drag my eyes open a crack. Just enough to see the disgusted and furious look the scarred man throws at his friend before disappearing up the stairs.

These men are capable of doing very violent and vile things. Yet, as the man with the kind blue eyes moves toward me, I'm not afraid of him. I finally give in to the fatigue my body has been fighting and let the darkness close in around me.

Something tugs at the iron loop on the floor holding my feet in place, then at the one in the wall restraining my hands.

"Fuck."

They made sure I was secured tightly. They had to. I was too valuable not to.

"I'll be right back."

The cool metal of the wall feels incredible against my warm skin. I sigh and give myself over further to the darkness. Something soft brushes against my exposed skin.

"I'm going to cover you with my shirt. I need to try to break this hook you're chained to from the wall, and I don't want you to get hurt by any debris."

His words barely register. All that does it how close I am.

So close...

So close to getting out of here.

Strong hands drag me away from the wall as far as the chains will allow and lower me down. The cold floor presses along the side of my body and face.

A loud series of clanks ring out, but I don't have the energy to investigate. I barely have enough to breathe at this point. Several more clanks resonate through the hold. The taut metal chain attaching me to the wall goes slack, but I can't move my arms. They hurt too much. Even thinking of moving hurts too much.

He shifts me to another place on the floor. More clanks and banging sound.

Then...silence.

All the chatter of the women has stopped. The rush of blood in my ears has ceased. The world has come to a standstill.

Strong hands grasp me and lift me from the floor. The momentary feeling of weightlessness makes my heart stutter.

The soft skin of a hard chest presses against my arm. Despite how warm it is compared to the air, I instinctually lean into it. I wrap an arm around his neck and cling to him with as much strength as I can find.

He is my lifeline. My only hope at this moment.

I finally give in to the thing that's threatened to drag me under for so long. The blackness. Instead of being bitterly cold and harsh, it's soft and welcoming. It cradles me and cocoons me inside it. And I let myself relax.

Because I have it. At long last.

Freedom.

I'll take it in any form.

3

ELIJAH

"**A**re you fucking insane?" Warwick sneers at me the moment my feet hit the deck of the *Calista*. His dark eyes flash black in his anger.

I adjust the woman who lies limp in my arms. She made an attempt to cling to me, but she passed out before I even made it up the stairs and onto the deck. Climbing down the ladder with one hand while supporting her challenged every muscle in my body, but I wasn't getting any help from her, and I wasn't about to let her fall.

War isn't wasting any time confronting me. He stands with his arms crossed over his chest, just a foot in front of me, blocking my path. His size and attitude have never been intimidating to me, but with this woman draped over me, I'm not in any position to fight him.

He scowls at me and points to my arms. "We're not taking her."

Cutter watches our showdown from his perch at the bow near the back of the *Destiny,* and Rion just takes it in from near the controls of the *Calista*. They don't appear to have any desire to intervene on either side of the argument.

I square my shoulders and take a step forward. "We are."

War shifts closer to me and fists his hands at his sides. "You want to take a kidnapped sex slave off this fucking ship? Have you lost your ever-loving mind?"

"I could've asked you the same thing when you took Grace."

His lip curls. I glance down at the woman in my arms. Her bare skin burns against mine even in the freezing cold air.

"She's sick, War. Really sick. She's not going to make it if we leave her here for the Coast Guard to find her. No fucking way. I'm not even sure she'll make it the half a day it will take us to get back to the warehouse."

He scoffs. "Great! So then, we'll have a dead body on our hands?"

"It wouldn't be the first one."

Cleaning up after Arturo's crew hit the warehouse several months ago took a lot of effort and a lot of bleach. But those men are now scattered safely at the bottom of Lake Michigan in pieces. If this one doesn't make it, we can always do the same with her, and Warwick knows it.

He's just being a dick.

"We're taking her." And that's my final word on the subject.

I don't ask these guys for much. Nothing really. The work I do with them is just like doing time again—sleep, cook, eat, repeat. Missions here and there in between. I lay low and try to stay out of their arguments, and I never ask for anything.

They can give me this.

If they don't, they're going to have a fight on their hands. My conscience won't let me leave her, but it will let me hurt them if they stand in my way.

Warwick takes another step closer and examines the woman. "Why her? There are five dozen women in there, according to what Cutter told me. What is it about this one?"

"None of those women helped us." I nod down at her. "This one did. And for all she knew, we were just as bad as the men who took her, or maybe worse. She risked her life and is continuing to risk her life by asking for help. I am not going to punish her and let her die if there's potential that we can help her after she helped us."

War growls again, a deep, low rumbling in his chest, and throws his hands up. "Fine, what the fuck do I care? It seems we have no rules or self-preservation instinct in this group anymore."

"Look who's talking." The retort slips out before I can stop it.

He believes taking Grace was the right thing to do and that it was our only choice back then. And maybe it was, but it led to a clusterfuck of epic proportion—one we're still trying to unravel—and now, we're about to have their baby added to the mix. So, my comment is warranted and true.

He can't argue with that.

I catch Rion's eye. "I'm taking her down below to get her in bed. I'll drive. I need you to look at her and do what you can while we're aboard."

He sighs and gives me a curt nod. "I only have my emergency kit with me. There won't be much I can do."

My arms tighten around the helpless girl. "I know. Just do what you can."

He shifts out of the doorway to let me pass. He isn't very happy about this development either, but he knows better than to question me when I'm like this. His medical training won't let him walk away from someone in need, either. Even if it pisses off War, Rion will try to save her.

I make my way through the cabin to the back bedroom and lay her across the king-size bed. She groans slightly, but her eyes don't open. Her long, dark lashes flutter across her cheeks, pink and warm with fever.

Every instinct in me tells me to cover her up, but when she's this feverish, being under the blankets would only make things worse...I think. Rion needs to be the one who makes those decisions. I may be the resident expert on women—at least the guys seem to think so—but he's the expert in the medical field.

Please don't be too late to save her.

I'm digging myself into a hole with the guys by demanding we take her. If it's all for nothing, it's only going to make things worse.

"I'm sorry I can't do more for you." I brush her sweat-dampened hair off her forehead. The soft skin there blazes under my palm. "We'll take care of you. I promise."

I move away from the bed and race up the stairs in time to see Warwick jump onto the *Destiny* as Cutter fires up the boat. War unties from us and tosses me one last angry look before disappearing into the wheelhouse.

Rion stands behind the controls. "I'll go look at her."

"I'll get us out of here." We're already fighting the clock to put as much distance between us and the dead bodies on that ship, and now, with her life hanging in the balance, too, things are even more dire.

He nods and moves to walk past me, then stops at my side. "Are you okay?"

Shit.

I don't know why he's asking—because of the men we just killed, because it's the Albanians, or because of that woman. Maybe all three. I don't have an answer for any of them. With Cutter or even Warwick, my immediate response would be, "*I'm fine.*" Rion and Preacher know better and can read me far easier. They're not as quick to accept my lies.

"I don't know." It's the truest answer I can give. And it'll have to do for now.

He sighs and wanders down the steps to the cabin. I fire up the *Calista* and pull away from the ghost ship that shouldn't be here, the one now littered with crewmembers' bodies and with a hold full of desperate women.

Leaving them has a lead ball sitting in my gut, but it's the only choice we had. We can't take them all on our boats, and even if we could, what would we do with them after that?

The best thing we can do is leave them here and get as far away as possible to call the Coast Guard. Preacher will ensure our broadcast can't be traced back to us, and they'll get the help they need—hopefully before anyone else comes down with whatever infection is attacking the woman downstairs.

It could be anything. The conditions down there were deplorable, and she could have been sick with this fever for days or even weeks. It may already be too late to save her life, but at least it won't end in that cargo hold. Someone will be with her in her final minutes.

Though, what comfort that actually offers is debatable.

Moonlight reflects off the dark, choppy water, and we race southwest toward civilization and the warehouse.

I grab the radio and call Preacher. "On our way back, plus one."

The radio crackles. "Warwick just told me. Need me to do anything?"

I run a hand back through my hair and clench my jaw.

Yeah, tell me I'm fucking insane to bring that woman with me.

But instead of saying those words, I just shake my head, even though he can't see me. "No, Rion's doing what he can right now, but as soon as we get there, I'm sure he'll pump her full of antibiotics and fluids until we can figure out what it is." Which is hopefully something easy to treat.

The last thing we need is for it to be something he can't control at the warehouse. We can't take her to a hospital, and exposing Grace to anything contagious would be catastrophic. "How far do you think we need to be before it's safe to radio the Coast Guard about the women still on the boat?"

"Give yourself at least five hours. Then, I can call from here. I've got voice distortion software and can reroute the signal so it looks like it's coming from anywhere in the world."

Five hours.

It's a long fucking time but not nearly as long as I thought we would have to wait. Still, the Coast Guard will take time getting to them way the fuck out there. That woman downstairs is still better off with Rion and us looking after her than waiting for the cavalry. They need to care for a lot of women. And the one downstairs is in really bad shape. The kind of shape that can't wait. I need to push this boat as hard and as fast as she'll go, or the woman who helped us could die.

If she does, I don't know if I'll ever be able to forgive myself. She begged me for help. She knew she was dying.

What if I can't save her?

I already have enough guilt to last a lifetime. Any more may destroy me.

Icy water sprays over the bow, and we make our way across the dark lake at what feels like a snail's pace. Rion finally appears at the stairs and makes his way up to me.

I glance over at him. The stern set of his jaw makes acid churn in my stomach. "How is she?"

He slumps into the chair next to the controls. "I slipped some aspirin under her tongue to dissolve and put cold, wet towels and a few ice packs on her to try to bring her temp down. It's one-oh-four."

"Shit. Anything else we can do?"

"Not much. She needs an IV and antibiotics that I won't have until we get to the warehouse." He heaves out a sigh. "Cold showers every hour. We can do that. And leave the ice packs and towels on in between. That's really it."

Someone needs to get in the shower with her?

That possibility had never entered my mind. But it makes sense. We need to get her temp down and help keep it down.

The thought of Rion doing it makes my heart twist in a way

it absolutely shouldn't. That girl is my responsibility now. I need to be the one to do it, even if it means putting myself in the agonizing position of having a dying woman in my arms again.

"Take the controls. I'll do it."

His dark eyes narrow on me skeptically. "You sure?"

No.

But I don't have a choice.

We need to keep her alive for the next ten hours or so. Long enough to get her to Rion's equipment and maybe figure out what her body is fighting so hard.

Then, we'll deal with the rest.

Like who she is and what to do with her.

4

EVANGELINE

For the first time in what feels like forever, something warm and soft cocoons me instead of the cold, hard concrete and dank, damp air of the hold of that ship.

A bone-deep ache weighs down my entire body, and I groan and shift slightly as I force my eyes open. They won't focus. The only light in the darkened room comes from a window across from me. Early morning light peeks from around the curtains drawn over it.

Where am I?

I replay the events that I can last remember.

The ship.

The men with guns.

The man with the scars.

The blue-eyed man with pain and sympathy in his gaze.

I begged him to take me with him.

He pulled me into his arms.

That man saved me.

I push myself up on my elbow, and a sharp bite of pain draws my attention to my right arm. An IV line runs from my elbow up to a metal stand beside the bed. My vision finally clears enough for me to survey the room.

The man who rescued me occupies a chair in the corner, his head dropped back, mouth slightly open. His chest rises and falls with soft, rhythmic breaths.

He's asleep. This must be his place.

I take in more of the room.

Walls of bookshelves.

A small table next to his chair with a chess set—game already started.

What looks to be a small closet and a dresser but not much else.

Where are we?

Every muscle in my body screams at me, and I push myself into a fully seated position. The bed creaks with my movement, and the man jerks awake. His eyes widen and focus directly on me. I glance down at myself. Someone put me in a black T-shirt that's far too large.

And nothing else. A sheet and comforter are the only things covering my lower body.

Did he undress me? What else did he do?

I clench my legs together, but there's no ache or pain there.

Thank God...

I don't think he hurt me. At least, not yet. I should be afraid of this man, keep my guard up all the same. Just because he took me from that ship doesn't mean he has good intentions.

He pushes to his feet slowly, flips on a lamp next to him, and treads halfway over to the bed. Concern twists his brow, and his gaze assesses me. "How are you feeling?"

"I..."

Don't know how to answer that.

It feels like I got run over by a truck. Every bone and muscle in my body aches. My head throbs. It's a real chore to even sit up. I can't remember ever being this exhausted before.

And this entire situation has unease settling in my chest. At that moment on the ship, when they were about to walk away and leave me, I thought these men were my way out, but they may just be a way into a whole new mess.

Where are we? And what are they going to do to me?

He shifts uncomfortably, waiting for my answer, and the muscles in his forearms flex, sending the tattoos there rippling. He's strong. Strong enough to hurt someone badly.

"I'll be right back." He disappears out the door without another look at me.

The door clicks shut, and I release a shaky breath.

What happened between the ship and here? How much time did I lose? What's going to happen now?

There are so many questions and no answers at this point. All that's clear is I need to keep up my guard around these men. I saw what they did. They know I'm a witness. That makes them as dangerous as the men who held me.

The door opens again, and a fat bulldog waddles into the room. The man who literally saved my life stands inside the jamb with a very pregnant redhead. He avoids looking at me, and instead motions toward her. "This is Grace."

She offers me a soft smile, and her pale green eyes radiate warmth. "Can I sit?" She points toward the edge of the bed. The dog jumps up onto the bed and sniffs and nuzzles me.

I peek over at my savior, who still stands frozen near the door. He doesn't offer me any indication of how I should be responding here or of what they may want.

Grace seems genuine, though, so I nod slowly and shift back slightly, closer to the wall and the corner the bed is pushed into.

What's this woman doing here with them?

She lowers herself to the bed with a grunt of effort and rests one hand on her massive stomach while she leans back and supports herself with the other.

The man glances between us and grabs the door handle. "I'll leave you guys for a couple minutes. Call me if you need me."

Grace nods at him then offers me a reassuring smile. He pauses for a moment, then he pulls the door closed behind him, leaving me alone with the beautiful redhead.

A silence lingers between us, and we watch each other. The dog seems unimpressed with the tension in the room and curls up at my side with a huff. The longer we sit, the stronger the urge to shift away from her becomes. Her gaze is too assessing, too filled with questions I may not be able or willing to answer.

What is she waiting for? Is she expecting me to say something?

She reaches out and pulls my hand into hers.

The move should send me scurrying back, but instead, her warm, gentle grip sends a reassuring buzz through me.

A long, slow breath releases from her lips. "I know you're probably scared right now, but these guys are not your enemy. No one here is going to hurt you. I promise. They look scary, but it's all an act. Well…most of it. What's your name?"

They're the words I needed to hear, and though I have no reason to, I somehow believe she's telling the truth. I believe they took me to help me, not to put me in a worse position or the same one they rescued me from. If they were really in the same business, they would have taken all the women, or at least the ones in the best shape. That they only took me—the one so weak and sick I could barely move—speaks volumes.

I push away my reluctance and clear my dry throat. "My-my name is Evangeline Manug. Eva." I scan the room again, but it offers little in the way of information. "Where are we?"

She squeezes my hand. "Somewhere safe. That's all you need to know right now. This is Elijah's room. He's the one who brought you here."

Elijah.

A name to go with the blue eyes and strong, tattooed arms.

"And this is Milo." She pets the dog for a moment. "You were very sick. You've been out for almost two days. You still have a slight fever, but it's gone down with Rion's treatment."

"Rion?"

She smiles again. "Sorry. He's another member of the crew. Army Ranger medic. He knows his shit. That IV has been in you since the moment they brought you in. He's been pumping you full of fluids and antibiotics because they weren't sure what made you so sick."

I close my eyes and picture the conditions in the hold of that ship. Something I never want to remember or relive, but it's so fresh in my mind, I can smell the crush of dirty bodies, the sweat, the panic, the desperation. Acid crawls up my throat, and I fight the urge to gag. "I don't know. A lot of us were sick at some point during the journey. It could've been anything."

There was a bathroom they occasionally let us use, but mostly, it was buckets. Showers and baths were unheard of, and they only fed us the bare minimum to keep us alive for the trip.

It was Hell on Earth. Not exactly the kind of place I imagined when I pictured fire and brimstone sitting in church during sermons, but our own *personal* Hell.

A shiver runs down my spine, and I wrap my free arm around myself.

She pats my hand, and when I meet her eyes, they soften and shimmer with unshed tears. "You seem to be doing a little bit better now, but I know Rion drew some blood, and he's having some tests run to make sure it's nothing more serious that needs a different treatment."

"Someone drew my blood when I was unconscious?" I glance down at my clothing again.

Grace's focus follows mine. She presses her lips together in a firm line and squeezes my hand again. "They didn't hurt you. They wouldn't. Elijah and Rion had to try to bring your temperature down on the boat ride back here. That required giving you ice-cold showers multiple times."

Showers?

"So...they saw me naked?"

She gives me a tight smile and shrugs. "I think only E did. He had to dress you in one of his shirts when you got here."

Like that makes it any better?

I tug my hand from between hers and wrap my arms around myself tightly, the cool air suddenly chilling my exposed skin.

"How would you like to take a long, hot shower and get cleaned up?" Grace's voice is soft and laced with genuine concern.

She's just trying to be nice and help me feel safe here. This is no act. No front she's putting on to get me to drop my guard.

I nod. The last time I took a hot shower...I was home. So long ago and so far away...

"The girls and I got some clothes together for you."

"The girls?"

She pushes off the bed slowly with a groan, holding her lower back. "Myself, Everly, and Valentina. They're the other guys' girlfriends. You'll meet everyone eventually. Rion is the big one. Preacher is the nerd next door with the beard and limp, and Cutter...well, you'll know which one he is. Milo is his dog, but he's a big softie and pretty much latches onto anyone who gives him food or any attention. Warwick is the head of the crew and this one's father." She rubs her belly. "But right now, just focus on getting cleaned up and feeling better." She pauses at the door. "And remember...you're safe here. I wouldn't be here if I didn't know that."

Her words are somewhat comforting, but at the same time, I thought I was safe back home. I thought I was in the hands of someone who cared for me and who would look out for me and protect me. I couldn't have been more wrong.

I need to be cautious if I'm going to survive this. "Thank you, Grace."

She grins and motions down the hallway. "The bathroom is at the end of the hall on the right. I put clean towels on the counter and some clothes in there for you. There are more over there." She points to a stack on top of the dresser. "Let me know if you need anything else. I'm sure E will be whipping up something for dinner soon."

Whipping up something for dinner?

I don't ask.

"I'll send Rion in to remove that IV so you can shower." She pauses and watches me. "Do you want me to stay for that?"

My heart warms at the offer. I have no idea who this Rion is, and she's willing to stay to make me feel more comfortable with the whole situation.

"No. I'm okay."

I think.

"Come on, Milo." The dog slowly lifts his head to look at her. His ears drop back, and she motions for him to come. He slowly lumbers to the edge of the bed and jumps down, and they disappear out the door. Grace closes it behind her, leaving me in E's inner sanctum with nothing but questions and no real answers. I have some names and empty promises. Nothing more.

The door opens, and a massive man with ink covering just about every exposed inch of his skin enters. He towers over me, and his sheer size and strength make me shrink back on the bed.

He holds his huge hands up. "Whoa. It's okay. I'm Rion. I won't hurt you."

That keeps being said, and while I want to believe the words, my recent experiences have proven what I want to believe and what is true are often two very different things. Grace seemed genuine, but these guys are another story.

His hands drop slowly. "I need to take out that IV if you want to get cleaned up."

God, yes, I do.

I nod and shift slightly closer to him. He takes a step toward the bed and kneels next to it with one palm extended. He sets a small container of medical supplies next to me.

My hand shakes, and I offer my right arm to him. He takes it into his hand, his rough hands gliding softly over my skin, and slowly removes the IV line. A tiny drop of blood rises to the surface. He presses a cotton swab over the spot and secures it in place with a piece of tape.

For such a huge man, he has a surprisingly gentle touch and bedside presence.

His dark eyes find mine, and he offers a tight smile. "I'll want to get you on some oral antibiotics now that you can take them. And depending on what comes back from the blood-work, we may have to change the treatment. You don't have any idea what you might have been exposed to? Is there anything I should be testing or treating you for?"

I know what he's asking. What he wants to know. What they all think happened out on that ship. The horrible, real trauma endured.

I suck in a breath through a sob. "I should be okay."

I'm not going to elaborate, and he doesn't push.

He squeezes my arm and pushes to his feet. "Go get cleaned up, then come meet us for dinner, if you feel up for it. Otherwise, we can bring you something in here."

"Thank you."

He pauses at the door and watches me for a moment. "You don't have to thank us for anything. What was done to you..." He trails off, and his empty hand tightens into a fist. He shakes his head. "You have nothing to thank us for."

He couldn't be more wrong.

They freed me from *that.*

But now...what?

I'm stuck in a foreign country with no family, no money, no documentation...what else can they do but send me back?

That isn't an option.

The thought of never seeing or talking to Ma and Pa again slices at my heart, but I don't have any other choice. I can't let it happen.

No matter what I have to do.

5

ELIJAH

"What the hell are we gonna do with her?" Rion takes a drink from his beer and raises an eyebrow.

The question comes from him, but everyone around the table is wondering the same thing—including *me*. And they're all looking at *me* for the answer. One I definitely don't have. At least, not yet.

Warwick's usual hard gaze focuses right at me. Cutter's typical sneer turns down the corner of his lip, and Preacher looks ready to jump on any information that might solve the five-foot problem currently showering in our bathroom.

They're all waiting for me to say something.

Which is problematic because I don't have a fucking clue what to do.

I shrug, trying to appear nonchalant without exposing how truly conflicted I am over having that woman here, especially without a plan. "She seems to be doing better."

Stating the obvious is about all I can come up with. Ever since she woke, and I saw her sitting up in my bed, wrapped in my T-shirt, I haven't been able to get that vision out of my head.

It's been a long, long time since a woman has been in my

clothes, let alone in my bed. I never thought it would happen again, and even under these circumstances, it's not anything I'm even remotely ready for. Neither was holding her small, shivering frame in my arms under that ice-cold spray in the shower on the *Calista*.

I almost completely lost it a dozen times and only managed to keep my shit together because I knew Rion couldn't take care of her and captain the boat at the same time.

Rion nods his agreement and downs his drink. "She's out of bed and cleaning up right now. I'll continue the course of treatment we've started unless something comes back in the blood tests to suggest we need to change tactics." He watches me for a moment. "But that doesn't answer my question."

I sigh, drop my elbows on the table, and scrub my hands over my face. "No, it doesn't. But I have no fucking clue what to do with her."

Preacher taps the table with his knuckles. "All we know right now is her name and that she's from the Philippines. I have some searches running so we can learn more."

Cutter throws up his hands. "Send her back. It's as simple as that."

Warwick turns to him, his brows drawn low. "How are we supposed to do that when she doesn't have a passport?"

"We drop her off at the closest embassy." Cutter's words are cold and emotionless.

I jerk my head up and glare at him. "She doesn't want to go back."

Her words on the boat were crystal-clear.

He slams his palm on the table. "Too fucking bad. It's not our responsibility to take care of her. We've already done more than we should have and put ourselves in jeopardy. She's now seen the warehouse and us. She knows our names."

His tone and attitude have my blood heating with anger. While his job may be to keep us safe and protected, his lack of empathy still manages to shock me even after all this time. "What the hell is she going to do? Who the fuck is she going to tell? We *helped* her."

His fist clenches. "That doesn't mean she won't turn on us the first chance she gets if it will benefit her."

I snarl at him. "That woman has been passed out in my bed for over forty-eight hours. She doesn't seem like any type of a threat."

If anything, her innocence and helplessness are unnerving.

Warwick groans and leans forward to rest his arms on the table. "We have enough to worry about without this girl thrown into the mix. We're still working to clean up this MC bullshit so we know Liz and Everly will be safe, and we need to watch out for any potential blowback coming from the Albanians now. We can't have her hanging around, too. It's just more trouble waiting to happen." His gaze darts over to me. "I think taking her to the embassy is a good option."

I scoff. "And do what? Just drop her at the front door in tire smoke?" I shove up from my chair and pace. "She doesn't have anything. No money. No ID. All we know is she doesn't want to go back. She's *terrified* to go back."

Those pain-filled eyes...pleading. The strangled words she could barely get out on that damn ship...

I grip the back of my chair and shake my head with my eyes clenched shut. "You should've seen the way she begged me, guys. It was almost like it was painful for her." I sigh and pinch the bridge of my nose. "We don't know what happened to her at home or what happened to her after she was taken. But if she doesn't want to go back, I'm not going to be the one who sends her someplace she doesn't want to be."

It feels too much like being an executioner. And I've already done far too much of that.

Cutter sneers at me again. "I don't care where she wants to be, as long as it isn't here. The embassy will sort everything out.

If there's really a problem with going back, they'll grant her asylum here, and she can start a new life."

Preacher gives me a sympathetic look and clears his throat. "I'll dig up what I can on her now that we have a name and a little bit of information. But I agree with Cutter and Warwick on this. Having her around here with everything we have going on isn't good for her or for us."

My chest burns with anger, and I dig my fingers into the wood of the chair.

They really just want to toss this poor girl out on her ass.

I can't do that to her. Not if there might be another option.

"What if we just *helped* her?" I read everyone around the table.

Preacher raises a dark eyebrow. "What do you mean?"

"I mean..." I pace as an idea forms. "What we did for Liz."

After we rescued Everly from the Roses and she filled us in on what happened to Liz, we tracked her down. The poor girl was hurt and terrified after what those MC assholes did to her. Understandably so. But Preacher gave her a new identity and a new place to live. A new life. At least, until she *wants* to come back. Until it's safe to come back. Which we've been working hard to accomplish.

Combining the information from Liz and Everly, we've been able to ID the bastards involved in Liz's attack and Everly's torture at the clubhouse. But we can't go back there again. They'll be ready for us next time. Preacher has already confirmed they've increased their security.

They may not know we were involved in the attack, but we're not stupid enough to try that a second time. Especially because there are innocents, members of the MC who didn't know what was happening.

This crew may be cold and heartless at times, but we do our best to only hurt those who deserve it. And we only have one more. The fourth was taken care of by us last week. We made it look like a drive-by. And we're almost ready to take on the final man.

Everyone stares at me, waiting for me to elaborate.

"What if we did for her what we did for Liz? We give her a new identity. Money to get her set up somewhere?"

The guys exchange looks around the table.

Preacher sighs and rubs at his beard. "I mean, we could... but it's a little bit different. Evangeline has never lived in the United States. This is a different country, a different culture, a different way of things working. We can't really just dump her out there in the world on her own."

Fuck.

He's right. That sweet girl would get swallowed up whole without someone to help her adjust to a new life. That would be almost as unfair as sending her back where she doesn't want to be.

I run a hand through my hair and continue to pace. "What if we put her with Liz?"

Warwick nods slowly. "It's not the worst idea. At least we could keep an eye on both of them. And if Evangeline ever does become a problem—"

I open my mouth, but he holds up his hand to stop me.

"Just hear me out, E. I know you don't think this girl is going to stir up any trouble, but we don't know that. She can ID us. She can give them enough information for any number of organizations to come after us, including the government. If we help her and put her up with Liz, she won't have any reason to turn on us. Theoretically."

Cutter snorts. "Theoretically. I don't like that fucking word."

Rion shakes his head. "Neither do I." He hooks his thumb back toward the hallway. "But we can't do anything just yet anyway. That girl seems pretty shaken. And she's still weak. She's still running a fever, and it's going to be at least another couple of days until we get the blood test results back. We need to keep her here so I can monitor her and take care of her for a while."

A little of the tension in my body releases. It's not that I want to keep her here any longer than necessary, but I don't want to shove her out on her own or even dump her with Liz so soon, either. She's been through enough trauma as it is. She needs somewhere she can feel safe, even if she can't stay here long.

Warwick taps the table. "Well, now that that's decided, we need to discuss our plan for tomorrow. We still on?"

Cutter pulls off his glasses and rubs his eyes before shoving them back into place. "We're good. This dude is like clockwork. Every Thursday at eleven. He'll be there."

War nods. "Good. So will we."

And one more piece of scum will be taken off the face of the Earth. One less thing to keep Everly and Liz and the rest of us awake at night.

Preacher tenses in his chair. His usually soft, kind eyes darken and harden, transforming him into someone else completely.

Warwick eyes him. "Do you want to join us on this one, Preacher?"

Ever since he pulled the trigger on Axle, Preacher has stayed away from the rest of the dirty work, and I can't say I blame him. Taking someone's life isn't something you can so easily get over, especially for a guy like Preacher, who already struggles with what we do and the kind of faith he has.

He wants them to pay for what they did and wants to ensure they can't hurt anyone else, but the need to handle it himself doesn't itch at him the way it would for War, or Cutter, or Rion.

Or me.

Preacher pushes to his feet. "No. You guys take care of it. Just make sure he suffers as much as Everly and Liz did." He walks away without another word, the weight of what happened to the woman he loves weighing heavily on his shoulders.

Warwick shrugs and glances around the table. "Then it's the four of us, like last time. As long as we stick to the plan and make it look like an accident, things will go fine."

We all nod our agreement. We've been planning this one for weeks. Cutter has each target's schedule down to the minute, and all it takes is the perfect opening for us to act. That opening just happens to be tomorrow for Vincent "Viking" Gorman.

Preacher reappears, his brow furrowed. "Guys, we may have a problem."

Warwick sighs. "Fuck. What now?"

"The news. They found the ship. A few of the women apparently mentioned men coming onto the ship to save them. They're calling us their *guardian angels.*"

Fuck.

6

EVANGELINE

The long, hot shower felt almost like a baptism. The months of filth and grime on my body and many of the tears and much of the anguish left in it washed away. Some of the tension in my muscles finally started to release. Constantly being on guard, always wondering when one of the men was going to come for me, it left me paranoid and jumpy, unable to just breathe. It feels like I haven't filled my lungs with pure, clean oxygen in so long, I've forgotten how to do it.

Breathe, Eva.

That's all I have to do now.

Breathe.

In and out. In and out. In and out.

I close my eyes and do it. The warm, wet air in the bathroom is thick but still the most magnificent gulps of air I've ever taken.

Just breathe.

Nothing more.

Just breathe...

And live.

Maybe it's possible. At this moment, living almost seems

within reach because I almost feel clean again, though whether that will ever truly be possible is another question entirely. After everything that's happened, that may be an unattainable dream. One that makes the dreams I had before look so damn naïve.

How could I have been so blind to what was really happening?

I swipe the condensation off the mirror in the bathroom to look at myself for the first time in weeks. My pronounced cheekbones protrude from my too-pale skin, and my soft hazel eyes, normally so bright, are flat and sunken into a face I barely recognize.

This isn't me. This isn't the happy, clueless girl I was back home.

But that girl *was* naïve.

That girl didn't understand the way the world worked. I was so sheltered from the world, from the dark and hard truths. Maybe it did me a disservice because I had no idea what was coming or that people could be so cruel. People who were supposed to be trusted. Looking back on it now, I wish I had known the reality of the world. It would have given me a warning. Perhaps a chance to save myself from all the pain and anguish. It could have let me develop the skill to read people, to see beneath the surface of their facades to their real intentions.

These people—at least the ones I've met, Grace, Rion, Elijah—seem genuine in their concern for me, but so did the last person who was supposed to care about me. Look what that got me. Look at what believing in the goodness of people did to me. It left me here, a shadow of myself.

Here. Like this.

I wrap my arms around my frail body, covered in someone else's clothes, and open the bathroom door. As much as I would love to hide in this warm cocoon away from the world in here forever, I'm exhausted and can't stay on my feet much longer.

The cool cement floor of the hallway tingles the bottom of

my bare feet. I tip-toe my way back toward the room where I woke.

Voices carry down the hall, echoing through what sounds like a large space. I peek around the corner into a vast warehouse with a massive ceiling that must be at least thirty feet high. Two boats rest in docks on the far side, and Elijah and Rion sit at the table with three other men in a heated discussion. One that looks intense and angry.

Ay punyeta!

I jerk my head back and bolt for the bedroom before they can see me. The last thing I need is them thinking I'm intentionally spying on them. Even though I want to know who they are and where they have me, I need to face the fact that they're in control of this situation. Anything that might raise their suspicions won't be good for me.

Not at all.

My body is still weak, and I have absolutely nothing here. There's nowhere for me to go. Nowhere I could run even if I were capable of doing that or I wanted to. I'm at their mercy. Utterly and completely helpless in all of this.

I close the door softly behind me and cringe at the click.

Please don't let anyone have heard or seen me.

I press my back to the door and hold my breath to listen for the sound of anyone coming. My eyes search the room, taking in all that I couldn't see very well this morning in the afternoon light now streaming in through the window. Someone pulled open the blinds while I was showering, and the new brightness exposes the starkness of the space.

Classic novels line the bookshelves along the wall. I cross the room slowly, taking a moment to scan the titles. My eyes drift down to the chessboard, and tears prick my eyes.

Something about the pieces spread out on the board reminds me of the game of life. So difficult. One I was never good at playing.

I swipe at my cheeks and move to the window to look out. Trees fill the landscape outside, each covered in white snow and crystallized ice. Sunlight glitters off them in a breathtakingly beautiful display that makes me shiver and wrap my arms around myself more tightly.

Winter. One more thing I know nothing about that I guess I'll have to get used to. The chill in the air. The lack of grass and flowers.

Will I ever feel the tropical heat again? Am I going to spend the rest of my life living with strangers?

Surely, they can't intend to let me stay here. I can't.

But where can I go? What can I do?

The tears fall in earnest now, and I cover my mouth to bite back the sob that threatens to escape. I drop down into the chair Elijah was sleeping in earlier today, lower my face into my hands, and let go.

Of all of it.

All the tension and anguish I didn't already unleash in the shower. Everything I've bottled up inside. Everything I gave up when I asked them to bring me here instead of going home. The life I can never have again.

But I'm not really giving it up when I couldn't have it back anyway, am I?

I just have to remember that. Remind myself of that fact every time things get tough, or I second-guess my decision to beg Elijah to take me with him. If he hadn't, I'd either be dead or in a room with the rest of those girls being questioned by some federal employees before being sent back to the people who put me here in the first place.

The door opens, and I jerk to my feet. My knee bumps the chessboard and knocks two pieces to the floor.

Elijah's eyes immediately dart to where they lie on the bare concrete. A tempest of rage explodes in his icy-blue eyes, and he thunders into the room at me. "What the hell are you doing? Don't fucking touch that."

He drops to his knees and grabs the pieces with frantic, shaking hands.

I cower back into the chair. "I...I'm sorry. It was an accident. I..."

"I don't fucking care." He roars at me, his anger a living, breathing thing that wraps around me and squeezes my throat.

"I...I..."

He pushes to his feet, his chest heaving in and out, his fury radiating off him in almost visible waves. "Don't fucking touch *anything* in here. Do you hear me?"

Footsteps echo down the hall. A tall, thin man with a dark beard appears at the door. His eyes flick between me in the chair and Elijah looming over me.

"E. What the fuck, man?"

Elijah's eyes widen, and he shakes his head as if to clear it and glances over his shoulder at the man in the doorway. "Fuck."

He runs a hand over his face, turns away from me, and makes his way toward the door slowly.

The bearded man grabs Elijah's shoulder to stop him.

Elijah shakes his head and stares at something on the floor. "I'm going for a run."

The man releases Elijah and lets him storm into the hallway before he turns back to look at me.

He enters slowly with his hands raised. "Sorry about that. I'm Preacher. We haven't met yet." He approaches cautiously and offers me his hand. "It's Evangeline, right?"

I reach out and accept his handshake.

His lips curl into a kind smile that matches the warmth of his gaze. "Ignore E. He didn't mean that. It wasn't about you."

I swallow thickly.

If that wasn't about me, what the hell was it about?

Preacher steps back and settles on the edge of the bed. He peers toward the door then back at me. "We're trying to work on a way to help you, but there are a few things I need to know."

I nod slowly.

He rests his elbows on his knees and watches me cautiously. "I was able to get a little bit of information to get things started, but I need you to confirm something for me first."

I nod again.

"You don't want to go back to the Philippines?"

I shake my head. He makes it sound so simple. "No. I *can't* go back. There's a difference."

He presses his lips together in a firm line. "I understand. And I'm not going to press you any further on that, but you need to know that if you're not going back, there are only so many other options left. You're here essentially without an identity. That's good and bad. It means I can make a new one for you, but there are some things we're going to need in return."

Did I hear him right?

"A new identity? You can do that?"

He nods. "We can give you a whole new life, but we need some things from you in return."

Of course, they do.

"Like what?"

He runs a hand along his beard. "Well, first...assurances."

"What kind of assurances?"

"That you're not going to rat us out. You know enough about us already to have the guys uneasy. And the longer you're here, the more dangerous you become to us."

Which is exactly what Elijah was alluding to when I asked him to take me from that ship. That maybe coming here wouldn't be any better than where I already was.

"If we help you, if we get you set up with a new life with

someone we trust who can help you, will you take it and be able to put all of this, including us, behind you without asking questions that we can't give you answers to?"

"Yes." The answer comes out before I even have time to consider what he's asking.

All I know is that it's an offer I can't turn down, no matter the consequences or repercussions that may come down the road.

They're offering me a new life. Even if the *assurances* can't be the only thing they'll want in return.

People don't do things simply out of the goodness of their hearts. There are always ulterior motives. Always things brewing beneath the surface. That's a hard truth I learned during all this.

So, while Preacher sits here offering me the moon and stars, all I can wonder is...

What else do they want from me? At what cost?

He climbs to his feet.

This all seems too easy. Something isn't right here. "Preacher?"

He turns back, and his soft brown eyes hold no hostility, only concern.

Maybe I misjudged him and the situation after all.

His brow furrows in concern. "What?"

"What else?" I hold my hands out. "What else do you need from me?"

He offers a slight shrug. "That's still to be determined. For now, just try to get better."

It seems easy enough, but it's far from it.

7

ELIJAH

"**I** don't like that look on your face." Cutter's voice cuts through the silence in my truck.

A silence I was enjoying. Asshole.

I glance over at him with a scowl. "It's dark outside. How the hell do you even know what my face looks like right now?"

Seriously, it's almost two in the morning, and out here, there aren't any streetlights or business lights to cast any sort of illumination into the cab.

What the hell is he talking about?

He snorts, shakes his head, and refocuses attention to using the binoculars to watch the building down the road and across the street from us. "I may be blind in one eye, but it doesn't take perfect vision to see that girl is affecting you."

"I don't know what you're talking about."

My answer may have come a little too quickly, especially for someone like Cutter, who is suspicious and analyzes everything down to every fucking minute detail.

The man is meticulous. It makes him brilliant at his job, but it's annoying as fuck when he turns that focus and those analytical skills on you. It's one of the reasons we all avoid discussing anything personal with him. Though, I don't talk about anything personal with anyone...

Typically, Cutter isn't one to launch into touchy-feely conversation, so the fact that he's bringing it up now means he's really concerned.

He leans forward slightly, changing the angle of his view. "You know you scared the crap out of her."

Shit.

I grit my teeth and try to forget the look on Evangeline's face when I lost my shit on her. "I know I did."

I scared the crap out of myself.

And afterward, I felt like a fucking asshole.

She didn't do anything wrong. After the hell she experienced, she needs to be handled with kid gloves, not bellowed at by an angry man who, for all she knows, is a violent psycho. She saw us come in and kill the men on the ship. She knows what we're capable of, and I scared the fuck out of her even more. All because I couldn't keep my shit together over a damn game.

Cutter sighs heavily and leans back in his seat. "You need to be careful, brother. We're walking a fine line with this woman. You piss her off or scare her too badly and the first place she goes when we set her loose is to the authorities. She's seen all of us long enough that she can identify us easily, and even if we blindfold her when we take her out of the warehouse, she's going to be able to describe the place and what she could see from the windows. Things like that. You get a smart cop and it won't take them long to zero in on us. And it's not like we blend well around here."

Now, it's my turn to snort and shake my head. "None of *you* assholes do."

It's ironic, really. I'm the only one with a felony record—and murder at that—yet I'm the one who everybody says looks like the boy next door. My tattoos are well hidden as long as I'm clothed, and my blue eyes and sandy blond hair tend to make me far less intimidating than the rest of the guys and their darker coloring.

But Cutter is right—Evangeline is a liability.

A beautiful one.

The moment I took her against everyone's wishes, I put all of us at risk. And then, when I walked in and saw her knock the pieces off the board, I gave her a reason not to trust us.

I shouldn't have lost my temper. She couldn't have known not to touch it, couldn't possibly know what it means to me, and I can't expect her to stay in bed and do nothing else until she's fully recovered and able to leave. If I didn't want her exploring and touching my things, I should have told her and not Hulked out on her.

That's Rion's thing. Not mine.

I hate to admit it, but Cutter's right about something else. She's a major problem for me. And not only because of what happened in my room earlier. Because she reminds me so much of *her*.

Sweet.

Trusting.

In need of love and protection.

And looking to me *for it.*

I clench my fists and shake off the images that have kept me awake at night for over ten years. The mix of joy and pain, anguish and love, agony and desire alternatively pull at me, tearing me apart from the inside out.

And Evangeline is making everything a hundred times worse.

Since the moment I saw her cowering and sick, chained to that damn wall in the ship, I knew I couldn't leave her. Even after Cutter told me to.

I can't and won't examine why.

Maybe I was naïve to think things would be better on the

outside. I thought it was bad when I was in the joint, when I had so little to distract me from what happened but the daily routine of living behind bars, but it's so much worse out here. Here, the reality of my life smacks me in the face every fucking morning when I wake and every night when I go to bed alone.

Seeing Warwick, Cutter, and Preacher find their happiness should thrill me. I should be happy for them. That they were able to overcome everything they've all been through to find that little bit of love and peace in the world.

In reality, all I am is angry. Angry that I lost it, and angry that I can never have it again.

But I can't let that cloud my judgment. Not tonight. Not ever. Especially not where Evangeline is concerned.

We have a job to do.

And that job just walked out of Smitty's Bar and over to his motorcycle.

Cutter pulls his Glock and slaps me on the shoulder. "Here we go."

I pull away from the curb, with Warwick and Rion in the SUV directly behind us, and head toward Viking as he fires up his bike. The man is completely oblivious to our approach down the road, and he pulls out onto the highway directly in front of us.

It's the perfect place for an ambush. Dark, desolate, and dangerous.

The drop off that runs along the left side of the road is three hundred feet straight down into the valley below. All it will take is one little nudge to send him careening over. And it will all look like an accident—like he was drunk and lost control, or a car came around the curve and ran him off the road.

A quick death isn't ideal, and it doesn't even remotely make him pay for what he did to Everly or Liz. He deserves to be raped and beaten and tortured the same way he did to them.

An eye for an eye.

But sometimes, the need for revenge and allowing wrath to take control of your decisions leads you down a road you can't come back from. I know that firsthand, and none of us are about to make a mistake that's going to get us sent away...or worse.

This end for Viking is necessary in this case.

After the way we took out the other fuckers from the MC, we have to be more careful about how we do the hits. We don't need them retaliating against us, and even though Everly is adamant there are good guys in the club who would probably do the same thing to the shady members themselves if they knew what really had happened, we can't take that chance.

So, while Cutter would love to use that gun on his lap, it's only a last resort. If we can make this look like an accident, all the better.

Viking reaches the curve in the road, and I gun it. The truck slams into the back tire of his motorcycle, and I push left. Warwick drives up alongside me on the right to ensure Viking can't veer back toward the road.

The bike wobbles and slams into the guard rail before coming back and hitting the side of my truck again. I push it left, and it smashes into the guard rail again. The metal gives way, and Viking has nowhere to go but over and down.

Cutter glances back toward the hole in the guardrail as we continue down the road. "Good riddance."

"No shit."

After the raid on the MC headquarters a few months ago, Preacher said the only way he dealt with the guilt of what he had done was to think of us as avenging angels sent to right a wrong. I could relate to that. And watching that fucker go over the side gave me the relief of knowing we're finally done with the MC.

The monsters who were responsible for what happened to Liz and Everly have all paid the price.

Now, it's time to focus on other things. Like the Albanians.

My hands tighten on the wheel.

After my experience with them, I shouldn't be so surprised they moved on to human trafficking. That they were capable of kidnapping women right off the street and making them do unspeakable things, of selling them to the highest bidder. It's definitely in their wheelhouse. Just one step beyond what they were already doing.

They may think they found a gold mine, but all they've done is put a target on their backs. One I'm ready to hit.

What they did to those women, to Evangeline, is the lowest of low. They aren't even human; they're fucking animals. Animals who need to be put down before they harm anyone else.

The guys are in agreement on that one hundred percent, but we need a plan. A way to remove them permanently without starting World War III and leaving Valentina at the center of a mob war in Chicago.

Things are already tense with the Rose Cartel since Val was forced to let them sell in her territory. Mr. Rose wasted no time cashing in on their agreement and getting his product out on the street, and Valentina can't do anything but sit back and allow it. It's the price she had to pay for getting Everly back alive. She's just waiting for him to make a mistake, to somehow violate their agreement so she can destroy him and have a reason.

We're already on the verge of one conflict. The last thing we need is a fight with the Albanians, too. We have to be smart about this. Just like we have been in dealing with the MC by taking the guys out one by one over time and in different ways, all untraceable to us.

If only it were that easy when it came to the Albanians. But they're a hardened, well-trained, vicious crew. Aleksander Gashi swooped in after his brother's death and made sure the organization was a well-oiled machine full of men willing to follow his commands without question.

I never would have taken him for the type to move onto trafficking, but maybe it's not that huge of a leap considering his headquarters were a strip club, and it was well-known his girls mostly came from Albania and other Eastern European countries. For all we know, maybe he was trafficking the whole time, just doing a better job at hiding it.

Either way, it can't continue, and we need to figure out a way to stop it. Fast.

And we need to get Evangeline healthy and out of the warehouse. Even faster.

If I'm going to keep my sanity.

Cutter's phone rings, and he glances at the screen. The scars on the right side of his face twist up with his grin. He pulls the phone to his ear. "Hey. Yeah, it's taken care of. We can meet tomorrow. You want us to come down there, or are you coming to us? Got it." He ends the call and glances over at me. "Valentina wants to meet to discuss the Albanian situation."

I grip the steering wheel until my knuckles whiten. "Good. Something has to be done."

Especially now that the girls from the ship are being debriefed by the FBI. Who knows how much they saw and are revealing about us.

"It will be. But don't let that girl get under your skin. We've all seen what happens when a woman does that."

8

EVANGELINE

What happened between Elijah and me has left me shaken, and while I'm sure Preacher's talk was meant to make me feel better about the entire situation, I'm more confused than ever.

Who are these people? And what do they want?

It seems *they* don't even know the answer to the second question, and I know next to nothing about them. Preacher's explanation about Elijah's outburst didn't really offer me much...other than more questions.

What could've happened to him that was so bad that he would go off on me like that over something so stupid?

That kind of anger over something so trivial must have an explanation. He was so kind, so gentle from what I remember of my rescue. He has been so careful to ensure I'm all right since I woke. His reaction was just overkill. There must be more to the story.

His room has offered me little in the way of insights into the man who saved me, but then again, I've been too afraid to really explore or dig into anything. Elijah's anger has made that even less likely. And even if I wanted to, I've been too tired and weak.

I've spent almost the entire time since Preacher left me in bed and in a half-awake, half-asleep state.

Rion swore I'll be back to one hundred percent in a few days, but I was in that ship's hold and sick for so long, this almost feels like being well, even though I'm definitely not back to how healthy I was before my ordeal.

I'm starting to get stir crazy in this room, but other than going to the bathroom, I haven't had the balls to venture out anywhere else. Even the small meals I've managed have been eaten in here, away from the prying eyes of these men and the questions that are undoubtedly running through their heads.

Maybe today is the day to take that step. To get up and venture out. To learn what I can about where I am and these people. Leaving this room is the only way I'll be able to rebuild my strength—physically and emotionally.

I can't hide forever. No matter how appealing that may sound at times.

I sit up and lean back against the wall, facing the room. My eyes immediately drift to the chessboard. The one that set Elijah off for no apparent reason.

It's so innocuous. A game. Yet, it brought out so much rage... and anguish.

That wasn't just about being angry. It was like I had reached into his chest and ripped out his heart.

I have so many questions. Ones he probably won't answer, and that's probably for the best. Knowing more about Elijah won't change the reality of the situation. I'm just as much a prisoner here as I was in the ship; it's just in a different way now. I'll have no say in what they decide to do with me. I'm at their mercy for everything—clothes, food, a place to stay. When it comes down to it, they own me as much as anyone who would have bought me from the Albanians.

That sends a shiver down my spine. This place and the apparent kindness of these people may have given me a false sense of security. Anyone capable of what they did on that ship is someone to maintain a healthy dose of fear of.

The door swings opens, and Elijah enters cautiously. A vise tightens around my chest. He didn't come back to the room last night, and he looks like he may not have slept.

Dark circles rim his red, bloodshot eyes, and he rubs at the back of his neck as he approaches slowly. He stops next to the bed. His gaze lingers on the small bruise from where the IV was in my arm and then slowly drifts up to meet mine.

Conflict swims in the fathomless blue depths of his eyes. "About earlier..."

"I'm sorry, Elijah...for whatever I did that upset you so much. I owe you my life. I won't touch anything else. I'll stay on this bed until..."

Until what?

I don't know.

Preacher suggested their ability to give me a new life, to set me up as someone else here.

Could I really do that? And can I really trust that they're going to spend that type of money and effort on someone like me for absolutely no reason?

It could just be a ploy to try to keep me cooperative while whatever the real plan is gets set in motion.

But the true turmoil Elijah seems to be in helps me push that away.

He's genuinely sorry for how he acted. He squeezes his eyes shut and pinches the bridge of his nose. "You shouldn't be apologizing. I should be."

Definitely not what I expected.

He trudges over to the chair next to the chess set and drops down into it with a heavy sigh. "I've never had anyone in this room before. I've never had anyone looking at or touching my stuff." He leans forward and rests his elbows on his knees, staring down at his clenched hands in front of him. "I spent eight years in prison with various cellmates and all that time watching my back and protecting my things."

Is that really what this is about? A reaction to wanting to protect his things?

I don't think so. There's something more he's not saying. Something he's holding back.

I swallow through a dry throat. "What's so important about the chess set?"

He looks at his hands for another few seconds. The knuckles turn white and shake with the force he uses to clasp them together. He draws in a heavy breath, and his eyes drift up to the small table the board sits on. He stares at it for what feels like hours but is probably only a few minutes before he finally lets his gaze move over to me.

The anguish there has my breath catching in my throat. There isn't anger anymore. This is pure, unadulterated agony.

He swallows thickly. "My wife gave it to me." His voice breaks, and he clenches his hands again. "A long time ago."

Wife? Elijah is married?

I glance at his left hand, but no ring sits on the all-important finger.

And if he's married, where is she?

The only women I've met or who have been mentioned to me are Grace, Everly, and Valentina. From what I can gather, they're in no way romantically involved with Elijah. A wife would *be* here with him. In this room. Her touch would be apparent. Her things would be easily found and seen.

But there's nothing feminine here. Nothing personal from her. Not a single photo or knick-knack. Not a throw pillow or soft blanket. Nothing I would expect to find in a room where a woman lives or did live in the recent past.

Nothing...

Except for that chessboard.

Whatever the reason for his wife's absence, clearly, the

chess set holds a deep connection to her. One that means something profound to him. It makes him seem so human, to know he cares about someone so much that he would be this upset. That he would apologize for how he reacted.

My heart goes out to him. "I'm sorry I touched it."

He pushes to his feet and shoves his hands through his hair roughly. The dirty blond locks fall into a disheveled mess, and he shakes his head. "No. Don't be. Really. What happened is on me."

The pain in his eyes hasn't dissipated and stirs something deep in my soul. I understand that kind of pain. I've experienced it. My bleeding heart has always been a weakness. One I never recognized until recent events. Maybe what has happened should act as a warning to keep me away from Elijah, but it's not in my nature to see someone suffering and not do what I can to help.

I slowly shift to the edge of the bed and stand on my weak, shaky legs. He watches me intently and with a hint of fear. I approach him with deliberate, cautious steps in the small space. He doesn't retreat, but his gaze holds a warning.

"I don't know what I'm supposed to be doing, Elijah."

"What do you mean?"

I wave my hands at him. "With you." I motion to the room. "With any of this. Preacher said you guys can give me a new life, but I don't understand..."

His brow furrows as he narrows his eyes on me. "You don't understand what?"

I throw up my hands. "Why? Why are any of you willing to help me? Why did you take me with you in the first place? I just don't understand."

Was it just a glimmer of the goodness deep inside him or something more?

His gaze softens. "You've never had someone help you just because it's the right thing to do?"

"Of course, but..."

All the people I knew in my former life, the one I can never go back to, helped me because they loved me. Or at least pretended to, for some of them. But these people, they have no reason.

He dips his head until my eyes meet his. "But what?"

"But you have no reason to help me. Unless you want something."

My conversation with Preacher didn't ease that worry. Elijah may hold the answer. He may be able to give some indication of what they expect from me.

His soft eyes harden, and he steps forward, closing the few feet between us. He reaches out slowly, giving me all the time in the world to retreat or raise a hand to stop him.

I should move away. I should be afraid of him being this close, this intimate.

Move, Eva!

But I'm frozen in place, unable or unwilling to back away from the man who only hours ago had me cowering and terrified.

He pushes a strand of my hair behind my ear. The warmth and roughness of his hand sends goose bumps skittering across my skin. I shiver, but it's not from fear. The move is so touching, so soft and gentle. A calm settles over me, one I haven't felt in the almost two months, since I was snatched off the street and awoke on that ship.

For some reason completely unknown to me, I trust Elijah. Even though he's offered me no explanations about who they are or what they'll do with me, even though he went into a violent rage over something I can't fully understand, even though I have no idea where he or the rest of the guys have been or what they've been doing, I don't think he'll hurt me.

This man rescued me from that hell. All he had to do was turn his back and walk away, back up those stairs, and never look back. I probably would have died down there, waiting for the Coast Guard to rescue us, and it would have been no skin off his back. He doesn't know me. He doesn't have any obligation, yet he took me and ensured I was well cared for.

There aren't a lot of men in this world who would do that without asking for something in return, and he seemed almost offended that I would ask what they're expecting from me.

A long silence lingers between us before he slowly pulls away his hand. "Don't worry, Evangeline, you have nothing to fear from us."

"Because you're the good guys?"

He barks out a laugh, and humor floods his eyes. "Oh, no, sweetheart, we are far from the good guys."

The confession should scare me, but it doesn't. Not when I've seen inside this man's soul to his true nature underneath the harsh exterior. His pain doesn't define who he is. It just masks what lies deep inside him.

He doesn't scare me.

That's where the real fear lies.

9

ELIJAH

Y ou're a fucking idiot.

I've been telling myself that for the last few hours since leaving Evangeline standing dumbstruck in my room.

And why wouldn't she be?

That can't happen again. I can't forget who I am, who she is, or where we are. The reality of the situation is she's leaving soon, and I'm far too broken to offer her anything more than a quick fuck. Given what probably happened to her on that ship, that's the furthest thing from her mind and from what she wants right now. Even if she did, I might not even be able to give her that. It's been so damn long, and she's not *her*.

What is it about that woman?

In all these years, I've never been so drawn to someone. So worried about what they think of me. So concerned over saying or doing something to upset them. I don't give a fuck what the guys think, and Grace, Everly, and Valentina seem to understand not to push me too far. But Eva...she's just so inquisitive. She may have been afraid of me when I lashed out at her, but she seems to know I won't hurt her. She *sees* me in a way no one else has in a very long time.

That's more terrifying than anything else I've ever faced.

I drop the final clean pot onto the drying rack next to the industrial sink a little too hard, then rest my hands on the counter and let my head fall forward, trying to stretch the tension out of the back of my neck and shoulders. Even half the day spent in the kitchen hasn't been able to clear my head.

"Jesus, E, what the hell is all the banging and slamming in here about?" Rion slides onto the counter and lets his legs dangle as he watches me.

Milo wanders into the kitchen after him, searching for anything we're willing to give him. He curls up next to the counter and watches us, waiting for his chance to strike on anything we might drop.

"Nothing." I push off the counter and grab a towel to dry the pot. "I'm fine."

"Sure, you are." The corner of his mouth tips up, and he crosses his arms over his chest.

Smug bastard.

"What's that supposed to mean?"

Rion is a never-ending source of annoyance and frustration. Always poking and prodding at us. Constantly getting into everyone's business and giving his advice, even though no one asks for it.

He's been smart enough to mostly leave me alone, but that has more to do with me almost killing him for asking too many questions when I first joined the crew than it does with anything else.

Everyone knows I prefer not to talk. About anything.

Silence is what kept me sane inside. Not getting involved in the gossip and the games prisoners play to occupy their time meant *my* time had less drama. Less drama was a good thing. Drama gets you killed in there. Except it also meant nothing mindless to occupy myself with during the long eight years—2,920 days. 70,080 hours. 4,204,800 minutes. 252,288,000 seconds. Nothing but time to think about what I did and what I lost.

It might have driven me to do something stupid, like try to take my own life if I hadn't had something to look forward to because of Warwick. I don't dare consider what it would have been like if I hadn't met him in the county jail before my trial. If we hadn't formed our friendship and if he hadn't stayed in touch all those years and offered me a job and a place to come when I got out.

Life would have been so different...if it even continued at all.

So, the fact that Rion is risking things coming to blows to poke at me speaks volumes.

I really must be fucked up.

He leans back with his palms on the counter and snort-laughs at me. "What's that supposed to mean? One word —Evangeline."

"Don't."

His eyebrows fly up in mock innocent confusion. "Don't what?"

I grab a spatula from the drying rack and wipe it then point it at him. "Don't go there."

He raises his hands in surrender. "I'm not going anywhere. Just making an observation that you've been pent-up and a little testier than usual since you carried a certain beautiful, sweet, Filipino girl up from the bowels of that ship."

I fist the towel in my hand and turn back to face him. "Do you want a trip to the hospital tonight? Is that what this is about? It's been a while since you beat the shit out of anybody. Do you just need a real good fight? Because that's the only reason I can think of you'd be pushing this topic of conversation."

He slides off the counter and smacks me on the shoulder. "No, man. I was just thinking it would be a real fucking shame if I ended up the only bachelor for life in this group." He moves toward the door. "And I came in here to tell you that Valentina arrived, and we're ready for the meeting."

"Why didn't you say that before instead of fucking with me?"

He shrugs and offers me that stupid grin of his. "What fun would that have been?"

I scowl at him and toss the towel onto the counter before I follow him out into the main warehouse area. Milo reluctantly follows us and heads straight for Cutter, who scoops him up onto his lap immediately. The guys all sit around the table, waiting with Valentina at the head, looking every bit the badass she is.

That woman is a true force of nature, and the way Cutter tries to pretend he doesn't turn into someone else around her always gives me a chuckle. The man is stupid in love with her, and even though the others may not see the changes in him, I sure as hell do whenever they're together.

Cutter will never be soft, but he gets the tiniest cracks in his hard exterior in her orbit.

She offers me a smile before I take up my usual spot. "I heard things went well last night."

I nod.

"Good, because now that that's over, it's time we address a much bigger problem."

Rion reclines in his chair with his hands behind his head. "Bigger than assholes who prey on defenseless women?"

She scowls at him. "Yeah. How about assholes who kidnap, rape, and sell the defenseless women?"

He grins at her. "Touché."

Valentina ignores him. "From what my sources have told me, it looks like most of the women from the ship aren't saying much. Whether they're too terrified or whether they're protecting you guys, I don't know."

I shrug. "Maybe a combination of both."

Valentina turns her attention to me. "They saw you take Evangeline, and you and Cutter were down there long enough that some of them could probably identify you."

"I realize that."

And I've been wondering when the FBI is going to knock down our door...

The woman who now heads one of the most powerful criminal enterprises in the country looks to Rion. "How is she doing?"

"Her fever broke, and I removed the IV. She'll stay on oral antibiotics and will continue to regain her strength and feel better over the next couple of days, but it may take a good couple weeks before she's really back to one hundred percent healthy. What happened to her isn't something you get over easily."

"No, it's not." I practically growl the words at him, and he flashes me that same grin he did earlier in the kitchen.

The man has no shame. Trying to turn my helping Evangeline into something more is a real douchebag move and completely out of line.

Valentina glances at me. "Have you talked to her?" She raises an eyebrow. "What does she want to do?"

I grab the back of my neck and shrug. "She says she can't go back, and I don't want to push her on why. Preacher explained what we can do for her, and it seems like she's a bit skeptical. But I think with a little bit of time, she'll come around. I didn't get the feeling she's going to rat us out to anyone."

She nods. "Good. I'll try to talk to her, too. Maybe she'll feel more comfortable speaking to a woman."

Warwick sighs. "She did fine with Grace, but she really shouldn't be out of bed if she doesn't have to be, so if you want to talk to her and maybe we can try Everly?" He raises an eyebrow at Preacher.

Preacher nods. "Given everything Everly survived, I'm sure she'd be more than willing to talk to her."

Valentina returns to her seat. "So that only leaves the issue of what to do about the Albanians. This is a major step up for them. A major change in their MO."

Warwick leans forward and rests his elbows on the table. "What do you think caused them to move to this?"

She shrugs and leans back in her chair. "From what *Il Padrone* told me before he was killed, these guys are not reckless people. Saban's death seems to have been somewhat of a fluke. He let down his guard around someone as lethal as Konstandin Morina and paid the price for it."

He certainly did.

Being beaten to death with a lamp in your own office is a pretty fucking epic way to go. And the fucker deserved it and then some.

Val's eyes darken. "Things changed when The Dragon arrived."

"Ohh *The Dragon*." Rion's sing-song statement gets dirty looks from around the table.

Warwick smacks his palm against the top. "It's not a fucking joke, Rion. The man was a monster."

That's putting it mildly.

Someone who can burn and flay people alive without an ounce of remorse isn't to be fucked with, which is one reason everyone has left the Albanians to their own devices in the last few years. No one wanted to tangle with Aleksander Gashi, for good reason.

Valentina nods her agreement to Warwick. "He definitely stepped up their operations, but I don't think he was involved in this. They've been bringing in girls for years, from Albania mostly, but from what I've been able to determine, it was all voluntary. They give them jobs, places to stay, sponsor their citizenship if possible. Some they brought in illegally, but as far as I know, there was no trafficking or prostitution happening."

I agree with her on that. They were never into that shit before. Everything else illegal, sure, but not *that*. I always found it humorous they suddenly had morals when it came to prostitution, but they could kill without blinking.

Kind of a strange place to draw the line.

Val taps her fingers on the table. "I think this was someone else. Someone working behind the scenes while Aleksander was still in control because this has been going on far longer than just since Aleksander died. The operation is too well oiled and too well planned for this to be their first run. This has been going on for longer than we know. Which means someone in the organization was doing it behind his back."

Cutter rubs at his jaw. "Who's the fucker stupid enough to cross Aleksander Gashi?"

That gets a chuckle from everyone, including me. I wouldn't normally show any humor when talking about these people, but we're about to plan a way to fucking eviscerate, so I let it slide.

Valentina scowls at Cutter. "His right-hand man stepped up when he died. Erjon Rexha. My guess is he either knew this was going on, or he was the one behind it initially, and he just ramped it up once he got the power."

Warwick sighs. "So, the question is, what we do about it?"

Rion claps his hands together once. "That's easy. We take the fuckers out."

Sounds good to me.

It's something I've dreamt about for a decade.

Valentina shakes her head. "It might not be that simple. I mean, look what happened when my cousin tried to take out my father."

Cutter snorts. "That was only fucked up because of you, *principessa*."

She scowls at him but ignores the jibe. "No. If we're going to take down this operation, we need to weed out who is involved and who knew about it before Aleksander died. We need to know who might be able to step up and take Erjon's place without keeping up this practice. We had a stable peace with them before, but after this interruption to their network, it won't be peaceful for long. We need someone on the inside."

Warwick nods. "I agree, but that's easier said than done."

Val glances over at me. "It might be...if we didn't have somebody who can walk right in the front door."

EVANGELINE

They're going after the Albanians.

My heart beats wildly, and I press myself even tighter against the wall in the hallway just outside the main warehouse where they're meeting. Thankfully, the vast open space means sound and voices carry and echo enough for me to make out what they're saying without getting so close they might see me.

These guys must be real badasses to be willing to take on people like the Albanians. They may have swept onto the ship and decimated that crew in minutes, but this will be different. This will be their entire organization in Chicago. And they aren't men to be messed with. I've seen what the men who took me were capable of. The resources at their disposal even just on that boat.

Guns.

Ammo.

Weapons I couldn't even identify.

They had it all.

I can't even imagine what that means the men in Chicago have access to. Elijah and these guys will be walking into a war with the deadliest of men.

Men who deserve anything that comes their way—there's no question. I've been praying for just that, for someone to rescue us and ensure those vile creatures get a taste of Karma. To ensure they pay for what they did.

But the risk to this crew, the things they might be facing makes acid climb up my throat. They can't possibly survive an assault like that.

Can they?

Elijah and his friends took out those men on the ship without a second thought, even before they knew what was in the cargo hold. Anyone who can do that is capable of doing some pretty vile things. The only reason I've let down my guard at all is that I have no choice.

And...these guys seem different somehow. Not softer, but their hard exteriors have cracks. Ones that can be exploited. Ones that can be pried open to let things slip inside. Things like love. Things like compassion. They may do their best to hide their weaknesses, but these women wouldn't be here with these men if they were unredeemable.

Grace and Everly got through to Warwick and Preacher, and the man with the scars—who must be Cutter—and Valentina seem to have their own unique relationship based on what I've seen during this meeting.

She may look more like she belongs on the runway in Milan than with this group, but they look to her almost like a leader. Like she somehow shares power with Warwick.

It's a strange dynamic out at that table for sure, and I've tried my best to watch them while remaining inconspicuous to try to get a better feel for what's going on.

All my eavesdropping has done is confuse me, though. It's hard to follow their conversation with no frame of reference.

Who is The Dragon? Who is Saban or Aleksander Gashi?

The names being thrown around mean nothing to me. The

only thing I've managed to grasp is that they *are* going after them. Soon. And it won't be an easy task.

Valentina looks over at Elijah. "It might be...if we didn't have somebody who can walk right in the front door."

What?

My lungs seize. I grab the wall to keep myself upright.

Elijah's face hardens, and his lips twist into a sneer that's visible even from where I stand. "No. Fucking. Way."

She reaches out to touch his arm, but he jerks his hand off the table.

Silence descends over the warehouse. You could hear a damn pin drop. The eerie calm feels like it's just the eye of the storm, and I brace myself for the deluge about to be unleashed when it passes.

Elijah shakes his head and squeezes his eyes shut. "You can't ask me to go in there."

Warwick runs a hand through his hair and stands. "We don't have a lot of options. We need to figure out what's going on, and we'll never get close enough otherwise."

Elijah scrubs his hands over his face and holds them there for a second. He looks back up, and his anger has been replaced with something else. *Fear.* "Even if I *would* do it...what makes you think they wouldn't kill me on sight."

Cutter sets Milo on the floor, pushes to his feet, and leans over the table. "They're under different leadership now. Maybe you can use that to your advantage. Tell them your beef was only with Saban."

Who is Saban, and how does Elijah know him?

There are so many names and so much information being tossed around, it's making my head spin. Though that may be more from the fact that this is the longest I've been on my feet in almost two months.

Elijah snorts, his jaw set. "Yeah, and if that doesn't work, I get a bullet to the fucking head."

I clamp my hand over my mouth to cover my gasp, but several heads jerk in my direction.

Ay punyeta!

If they catch me spying on them, things likely won't end well for me.

I plaster myself against the wall and race back to the relative safety of Elijah's room.

What is going on?

It sounds like he used to be one of them. One of the Albanians involved in the human trafficking ring that was holding me.

How could he ever work with those monsters? How could he ever be involved with something so heartless and ruthless? How?

For one brief moment, it sounded like retribution would be coming to those who did something so awful, but my mind can't wrap around the fact that the man who brushed my hair from my face so gently, whose eyes are so full of pain and anguish could be one of them...

It certainly changes things.

They said they need to know what's going on in the organization, that they can't even begin to think about striking without that knowledge. I was so close to giving them all the information I gathered over our many weeks at sea, but now...

That's all information I should probably keep to myself. Hold onto it as a bargaining chip in case these guys ever turn on me or finally come to collect whatever it is they really want.

I need to protect myself—my body and my heart. I can't let this man slip through my defenses just because I feel a strangely intense attraction to him and am drawn in by his pain.

We are not the same.

Whatever caused the darkness in his eyes is not the same as what happened to me. I just have to remember that if I want to stay alive. He's been damaged in a way that may not be fixable.

The door opens, and I jerk around to face it. Dim lighting from the hallway shines in around Elijah, and he steps through the door with a tension in his body so similar to how he looked right before he went off on me before.

Elijah narrows his eyes on me. "How long have you been awake?"

I retreat across the room, moving away from him until my back hits the wall next to the single window. "I-I...just a few minutes. I had to use the bathroom."

He stops his advance halfway across the room and surveys me like he's searching for the lie.

I've never been a particularly good liar. It was always drilled into me that it was a sin. For so long, the fear of burning in Hell for a little fib was a real possibility, and even as I've grown older and come to question a lot of those beliefs, I still can't shake the feeling in my gut when an untruth slips from my lips.

Elijah takes a step toward me, and then another. "Are you lying to me?"

I open my mouth to lie again, but the words won't come out this time. Sweat breaks out on my brow, and my legs shake as he moves closer.

When did it get so hot in here?

He stops a few steps from me. "Tell me the truth, Evangeline. Were you listening to our meeting?"

Ay shet.

With his huge body towering over me, blocking my means of escape, my heart rate surges. My chest tightens. Blood rushes and thrums in my ears, blocking out all other sounds. Darkness encroaches on my vision, and Elijah blurs in front of me.

"Evangeline?"

My name is garbled. The room spins. I reach out for something, anything to grab onto.

Strong arms wrap around me and hold me up.

"Evangeline? Are you all right? Just breathe."

I suck in a shaky breath. My chest rises and falls slowly, and with each little bit of oxygen, my vision starts to refocus. His hard, warm body presses against mine, and his arms tighten. He walks me over to the chair and eases me down into it.

What just happened?

Concerned blue eyes search mine, and he squeezes my knee with his large hand. "You okay?"

I nod slowly. "I think so."

"You want to tell me what just happened?"

The fact that he hasn't removed his hand from my leg draws my attention to where our bodies touch.

It's not sexual. It's comforting.

He's concerned about me. Genuinely worried. So am I. Nothing like that has ever happened before.

"I'm not sure what happened. I couldn't breathe. Everything kind of blurred."

He squeezes again. "It looked like you had a panic attack. After I asked you to tell me the truth." He pauses and runs his free hand over his stubbled jaw. "Which leads me to believe you were listening."

There's no way around the truth. My own body betrayed me.

I suck in a deep breath. "Yes. I heard some of it."

His light eyebrows rise. "And..."

"And now I'm even more confused about who all of you are and what you were doing out on that boat. And about what you want from me."

He sighs and drops his head for a moment before meeting my gaze again. "There are a lot of things I can't tell you. A lot of things that you're better off staying in the dark about. Just know that we don't mean you any harm. You don't need to be afraid..." He glances back toward the warehouse and chuckles to himself. "Well, at least not of most of us. Cutter can be a real asshole and harsh, but he would never lay a hand on you."

"Is he the one with the scars and sunglasses?" It's the only logical deduction based on what I've seen and heard.

Elijah nods, and a tiny smile pulls at his lips. "What gave it away?"

That draws a laugh from somewhere deep inside me that hasn't come to life in so long, I can't even remember it. "He's kind of an asshole, huh?"

"That's putting it mildly." He pats my leg and pushes to his feet. "Really, Eva, you don't need to worry about anything other than getting better."

A question lingers on the tip of my tongue. One I should be too scared to ask but am too interested not to. "Are you one of them? The Albanians?"

His body tenses, and he clenches his eyes shut. "No. But I knew them and worked with them a long time ago."

"And you and those guys out there are going to take them out?"

He squats in front of me again and meets my eyes. "We're going to do everything we can to make them pay for what they did."

The sincerity and promise in his statement goes straight to my heart and sends a warmth spreading through my body. "Does it mean you have to go in, like Valentina suggested?"

Something dark and painful crosses his eyes. Something I recognize all too well.

Resignation.

He doesn't want to do it. Going in will be agonizingly painful. It will kill him to have to do it. But he's going to anyway.

"I think it does."

11

ELIJAH

The once-familiar thrumming bass of the sultry music vibrates in my chest before I even pull open the door. I never thought I'd be back here. Not after what happened. Not after all this time.

Yet here I am, walking into the lion's den. And given my history with the Albanians, I might as well have a slab of raw meat strapped to my back.

"We're good, E." Rion's whispered words behind me don't offer the comfort I'm sure he hopes they will.

They're really nothing more than a platitude to try to keep me calm. He doesn't know shit. He certainly doesn't know we're "good."

But at least I'm not going in alone.

Obviously, having Cutter join me would be the best play. He's the most lethal, the best trained, the most observant, but he's also the one most likely to cause trouble.

People see the scars and the glasses he refuses to take off. They see the way he carries himself...and they know. They know what he is. They know he's dangerous. They know he's not someone to fuck with, and when it comes to the fuckers in this club, they're more likely to take us out before we can ask any questions if they see him.

Rion, on the other hand, has a congenial disposition that seems to put people at ease despite his massive size. Let's just hope he doesn't flip a switch and Hulk out because then, we will be seriously fucked. He hasn't done it in so long—since he hit that dude on the *Neptune's Daughter* when we took Grace—it would be easy to think it's unlikely to happen. But with Rion, it's always within the realm of possibility.

I step into the dim light of the club, and the familiar scent of stale smoke and beer, cheap body spray, and sweat hits my nose. A girl with long dark hair dances on stage and wraps her leg around the pole. Her breasts sway heavily with her every movement, and she locks eyes with me and grins.

I'm sure I don't know her. They don't keep women around here very long. Definitely not ten years. And that's probably the last time I set foot in here.

Ten years.

Ten.

Fucking.

Years.

Not long enough. I wish this place, and anywhere else those fuckers have their hands in, would have burned to the ground long ago.

I work my way over to the bar as casually as I can, keeping an eye on the other clientele as I pass. I catch Rion doing the same. Almost every man in here is connected in some way—whether at the street level, by blood, or by loose association. This isn't a place you just walk into without knowing someone or being invited.

And we sure as shit weren't invited.

Rion claps me on the shoulder. "Man, I'm ready for a drink and some pussy."

I would think he's just joking around and playing a part to

put anyone who might be watching us and who is within earshot at ease, but the truth is, bars are like crack to Rion and throwing naked women into the mix is just recipe for a bender.

One I have no desire to participate in.

No one can keep up with the big guy when he drinks, and no one wants to try. It's the easiest way to end up in the hospital with alcohol poisoning or dead on the sticky floor of a dive.

We find two empty stools at the bar and slide onto them as the song winds down. The half a dozen other guys in the place clap, and a new song starts up. A petite redhead takes the stage, her high, small breasts barely large enough to move much. The deer in headlights look in her green eyes makes acid crawl up my throat.

She must be a newbie.

I feel bad for the poor girl. She probably wanted a new life and opportunity in America and had no idea what she was signing up for. Especially if it's true that they never included prostitution or trafficking in the past. She could be one of the women off an earlier boat, just like the one we took Evangeline from.

"What are you two having?" The bartender on the other side of the grungy wooden bar eyes us suspiciously.

Rion wraps his massive arm around my shoulders. "I'll have whatever you have on tap, and my boy here will take a Jack Daniels neat."

I scowl at him. He knows I have almost no tolerance left after being sober for so long. If I drink the hard shit, I will be flat on my face in an hour.

Moron.

We don't need anything dulling our senses right now.

I shake my head. "I'll have what he's having."

The bartender nods and walks away to fill two steins but keeps his eyes on us the whole time.

He doesn't look familiar. Definitely not someone who was

here the last time I was, but he's smart. We're strangers, and he already senses something is off. This isn't the kind of place you wander into off the street. You only find it if you come looking.

It won't do us any good to have him suspicious.

It's time to throw out the only bargaining chip I have.

He comes back over and sets the beers in front of us. "Cash or do you want to open a tab."

"Cash." Rion grabs a twenty from his wallet and smacks it on the bar. "That cover it?"

The bartender glances down and then chuckles. "That'll cover four more for each of you. It's happy hour—two-dollar beers."

Rion flashes a grin. "Sweet. Keep them coming."

"You got it." He knocks on the bar, slides the cash into the register, and turns to walk away.

It's now or never.

"Hey, excuse me."

He turns back around. I motion him over and lean forward across the bar. He does the same with a glint of reservation in his hard stare.

"Say, I used to do a little work for Saban back in the day."

His eyes widen slightly, and he looks me up and down. That scrutinizing gaze lingers on the tattoo on my chest I made sure would show with my top couple of buttons undone. "Is that so?"

I nod and pull up my long sleeves slightly, exposing the ink on my forearms. "I know he and Aleksander are gone. I'm just curious who's running the joint now."

The joint. Make the question about the club, not about the whole enterprise. It makes the question less suspicious.

In theory.

He presses his mouth together in a firm line and shakes his head. "Not sure what you're talking about."

I motion around me. "This place. Who runs it now? I might be looking for some work again."

He narrows his eyes on me, and his gaze flicks over to a big man sitting at the end of the bar. "We're not looking to hire anyone right now."

The guy who looks like a linebacker stands from his stool. Rion tenses next to me but still raises his glass to his lips and downs half the beer. He's ready for a fight if we need to, but he knows not to make a move until absolutely necessary. This may be our only shot to get an "in" and find out what we need to know.

"Look," I try to keep an eye on the bartender and the huge man slowly moving toward us simultaneously, "just give my name and number to who it needs to get to. That's all I ask."

I hold my breath while I wait for him to make a decision. Sweat beads along my brow, and I curl my hand around the cool pint glass to have a weapon should I need one. There's no way I'll have time to pull my gun before one of the guys in here shoots us up. The bartender clenches his jaw and surveys me again, then raises a hand toward the big man, telling him to stop.

Fuck. That was close.

My fingers slowly uncurl from around the glass, and the bartender slides a napkin and pen over to me.

I scribble my name and number on the thin paper and push it back to him. He grabs it while I take a long pull at my beer.

His brow rises. "Elijah Swift?"

"That's me." I take another drink and glance at the end of the bar, where the big guy still watches our exchange intently. "Can you make sure it gets to who it needs to get to?"

He rubs a hand over his jaw and nods. "Yeah, I can do that." He shoves the napkin into his pocket. "How long you been out?"

Ah ha. He does know who I am...

"Long enough that I'm ready to get back into the game."

He offers a nod then moves to the end of the bar to talk to his massive friend. The larger man eyes me, and the bartender hands him the napkin. He reads it then rises and disappears down the hallway that leads back to what is no doubt the office of Erjon, the new head of the organization.

Rion leans back against the bar and focuses on the girl on the stage—a brunette now. At least, that's what it should look like he's doing to anyone not trained to know the reality. He's keeping an eye on everyone and facing any would-be attackers while I watch the bartender and make sure he's not reaching for a weapon.

I sip at my cool, cheap beer and try not to look like I'm about to crawl out of my skin. This shit was never my forte. Waiting. For anything. But especially waiting to see what side of the line things are going to come down on—walk out alive or end up in some back room riddled with bullets.

The former would be preferred to the latter, but they'd be completely justified in dragging us down that hallway and disposing of us in a not so friendly manner.

After what I did, I didn't exactly expect a warm reception.

Rion nudges me with his arm. "The brunette is sexy as hell."

I glance at the woman wrapped around the pole and shrug nonchalantly. "I guess."

"You guess?" Rion scoffs and shakes his head. "Not as hot as a certain girl currently sleeping in your bed, though, right?"

Jackass.

I turn on the stool to face him and grit my teeth to keep from starting a fight with *him* when we need to be watching our backs for these Albanian fuckers. "Evangeline is beautiful. But she's broken. That woman just went through hell. Show some damn respect."

Rion's eyebrows shoot up. "Whoa." His hands raise in surrender. "Chill, E."

Chill?

For as much as I love the guy, Rion has really been grating on every last nerve I have since Evangeline arrived in our lives. He has no shame. The last thing that girl is looking for is to start up something with a man like me.

What kind of a life can she have after what those bastards did?

I've been asking myself that question since I first looked down at her in my arms on that ship. I may have saved her life, but that doesn't mean she's going to be okay. I know first-hand that just because your heart is beating and you're drawing air into your lungs, that doesn't mean you're living.

Our reluctantly friendly bartender returns and nods toward the door. "I think it's best if you two leave."

It's been at least ten minutes since the big guy disappeared down that hallway. I would have expected a response by now, but the warning from the bartender is enough for me to know it's time to go.

I slip off my stool. "Thanks for your help."

Rion raps the bar with his knuckles. "And the beer. Keep the change."

If Erjon is going to take the bait, it won't be immediately. These are the type of men who keep people waiting just to prove they have all the control. It could be days or even weeks before I hear from him, if at all. Which means we may have to move forward without any additional information. A tactic that always leads to bad fucking news.

Which is what we would probably be facing if we stayed here any longer given the looks we're getting from some of the "patrons."

Let's get the fuck outta here.

12

EVANGELINE

"I'm really glad you told us." Valentina glances at Everly before bringing her attention back to me. "But I think you should tell the guys."

I pull my hand from where it rests between hers and shift on the bed until my back hits the wall. "No." I shake my head and blink away the burn of tears trying to form. "It doesn't matter. They don't need to hear the whole sordid history of what brought me here. All that matters is, I can't go home."

Valentina presses her lips into a thin, hard line and pushes to her feet. She wanders over past the chessboard and drags her finger along the edge of the bookcase as she scans the titles. "We all have secrets, Evangeline. Some more than others. Things we don't want anyone to know, even those closest to us." Her amber eyes drift over to me. "When I was first introduced to these guys, Grace told me that every one of them has a story to tell but that it was theirs to tell. I've always respected that. So, we won't reveal anything you told us, even though I think it's important that they know. Right, Everly?"

Everly forces a smile that doesn't quite touch her kind eyes and nods. She gently runs her hand over Milo's back, and the dog soaks it up, releasing a little contented huffed breath. "I won't say anything, but I agree. I think you should tell them. If they understood why you don't want to go back, they might not be so concerned about what's going to happen with you once all this is over."

When the girls came in to check on me, I thought it would be another quick thing and I'd be left alone in here again, wondering what my life is going to be and why I can't stop thinking about the man with the haunted blue eyes who rescued me. I certainly never expected them to sit down and for Everly to tell me about her tortured past.

She suffered so much. And for so damn long. Two years of constant abuse and living in fear every second. It's so much worse than what happened on that boat in so many ways. It's what could have been my future if Elijah hadn't brought me here.

But I also understand the concerns they brought with them. *How could I not?*

Everyone is wondering why I won't go back and what I intend to do once I leave them. I can understand that. From what the girls told me, the authorities are diving right into an investigation into the women found on the ship, and we have no way of knowing whether anyone told them anything about the guys that could lead the authorities here, or about me and that I was taken.

This could all get very messy for them if I ever went to the authorities. And since my blood tests came back clean, and I'm finally healthy, the day I can leave is not so far in the future.

I run a hand across the bedspread under me and sigh. "I told you before. You don't have to worry. All I want is a new life. If the guys can really offer me that, then I'll be gone, and it will be like I was never here."

Valentina snorts and shakes her head, sending her long, glossy black hair swaying. "I doubt that very much, *cara mia.*"

Everly just smiles.

I glance between them, searching for some explanation. "What's that supposed to mean?"

Val returns to the bed and sits on the edge next to Everly. "You've made quite the impression on Elijah."

What? How could she know that?

Unless everyone knows about our confrontation. The way he flipped out on me.

How embarrassing.

"Yeah," I nod, "I really have managed to piss him off."

She chuckles and shakes her head while she pats me on the knee. "That's not what I meant."

Then what did she mean?

Every time Elijah and I are alone together, things just seem to get so...tense. And complicated.

This is a man who has seen me naked. Who held me in his arms while I was unconscious and took care of me just because he thought it was the right thing to do. A man who stirs something in me with the simplest touch yet can also terrify me with a single look.

Everly reaches out and takes my hand. "I think you should tell E what you just told us. And maybe he'll tell you his history. I know you must be curious."

I bite my lip. I'm not about to admit I want to know what makes him tick, that I want to understand how he can go from so gentle and caring to so angry in a moment, or why this entire situation seems to have him on edge.

"I'll think about it."

It will have to be enough for them right now because I have no desire to reveal the truth to any of the guys, especially Elijah. He'll think I'm a naïve fool. A stupid love-struck girl who knows nothing about the world or how it works.

And he might be right.

Valentina and Everly both nod, and voices echo in the warehouse. Milo jerks his head up and turns toward the sound.

Everly glances over her shoulder toward the open door. "It sounds like E and Rion are back."

"Back? Where did they go?"

The girls exchange a look then forced smiles.

"It doesn't matter." Everly pushes to her feet and disappears out the door with one final glance at us.

Valentina leans into me like she's about to whisper some deep, dark secret into my ear, even though we're the only ones in the room. "Check the second book on the top shelf."

I jerk my head back from hers. "What?"

She nods toward the bookcase behind the small table with the chess set before she stands and hustles out the door without another word.

What is she talking about? Is she saying I should look at the book?

I glance at the open door. Voices trail in from the warehouse, but it sounds like everyone is out near the table and not down here by the bedrooms. Milo drags himself up and jumps from the bed to check out whatever is happening outside this room.

Curiosity tickles the back of my brain.

Why would Valentina want me to look there if it weren't important? What is she trying to tell me?

I slowly inch off the bed. The concrete floor chills my bare feet and sends a shiver up my spine. Though it may be the sneaking around. I pad my way across the room, glancing over my shoulder toward the door with every step.

A strange mix of fear and anticipation has my heart thundering and blood rushing in my ears. I've already seen how E's mood can swing faster than the weather, and I don't want to be caught prying into things he wants me out of.

But I can't help myself.

I push up onto my tiptoes and peek up at the top shelf. The book Valentina mentioned is pushed back from the front edge, and my fingers can barely brush it.

Crap.

It's too far back. I should just let it go. Whatever Valentina wants me to see can wait until Elijah is willing to show it to me. I drop back down and stare up at it. The empty spine doesn't offer any hint as to what the pages might hold.

Walk away, Eva.

I chew on my bottom lip and glance at the door again. There still isn't any sign of Elijah. My eyes drift back to the book.

Shit.

There's no use. I won't be able to think about anything else until I know what's in it.

I shift up onto my tiptoes and manage to run my fingers around the edge and drag it out. The plain, dark-brown leather binding seems innocuous enough. I flip open the first page and my heart stalls. My breathing stops.

A beautiful brunette smiles at me. Laughter and love sparkle in her gaze. Her hand rests against her swollen pregnant belly.

I swallow against the sudden dryness in my throat and flip the page with a shaky hand. Another image of the same woman stares back. The smile in this one is more reserved as she leans back against a tree trunk, hands on her belly.

It's a pregnancy photo album.

I turn the next page, and tears sting my eyes. One slowly trickles down my cheek as I brush my finger over the photo of a much younger Elijah with his arms wrapped protectively around the woman with his hands resting over hers on her belly.

His wife.

She was pregnant.

Where is she, and where is that baby?

Page after page. Photo after photo. Each one shows love in the soon-to-be family.

Elijah looking into her eyes. Elijah kissing her. Elijah touching her belly, where his child grows. Elijah so in love...

No...

The tears flow freely now as do the questions.

He's not the same man as he was in these photos. The man who rescued me is jaded...angry...volatile. But also, kind and thoughtful and full of turmoil. Two different people in one.

What the hell happened?

"Eva..."

My name floats across the room, rolling off Elijah's tongue in a low, gravelly tone.

I jerk up my head, and the book clatters to the floor.

He stands just inside the door, hands fisted at his sides.

Every hair on my arms stand on end. "I'm sorry. I didn't mean to pry. I..."

That's a lie.

I was prying. It's exactly what I was doing.

And Elijah knows it. Even after our earlier confrontation, I just couldn't keep my desire to know more about this man from making me do something stupid.

I expect him to fly off in a rage. To scream at me for invading his personal space and items again, but he just stands there with his fists at his sides and his jaw clenched so tightly that a muscle in his jaw tics.

He sucks in a deep breath and closes his eyes briefly. When they reopen, they connect with mine, and it's like watching a hurricane swirl in their blue depths. "She's dead."

Dead?

It's such a simple explanation that brings so many more questions.

Do I risk asking?

Given my track record since I arrived here, I don't think it's possible not to.

"How?" It's barely a whisper, one that burns coming across my lips, but even from across the room, he hears it.

He stiffens, and his eyes darken even more, shifting from a swirling hazy blue to an almost midnight color. He steps closer to me slowly, his fists opening and closing at his sides, a vein straining on his neck. "You don't want to know what happened, Eva."

"Please..." I reach up and wipe away the tears from my eyes. "I do."

I need to know.

He shakes his head and stops a few feet from me. "You. Don't. Want. To. Know." Each word slips from between gritted teeth with such force, they move me back a step.

But he won't scare me or dissuade me from finding out the truth. Not now that I've seen part of it with my own two eyes.

"I wouldn't ask if I didn't want to know, Elijah. I'm just trying to understand this." I motion to the book on the floor. "Understand you."

He swallows thickly and squats to pick up the album. The silence and stillness in the air weigh down on me like a thousand-pound anvil. He stays down there, the book open in his hands to a photo of his wife lying nude with her legs crossed and her hands covering her breasts, her swollen belly exposed. He brushes his fingers reverently over her for a moment, and every remaining piece of my heart shatters.

His pain is palpable—a living, breathing monster occupying every available inch of space in the room with us and threatening to swallow him whole and suck me right down with him.

I inch forward, my hand out. He slams the book shut and shoves upright so fast, I stumble back.

He pushes the book into its place on the shelf and turns to

face me. "My life and my past are just that. Mine and in the past. It's not something I talk about or want to remember." Pain causes his words to shake, and the tension in his shoulders looks ready to snap him in half.

Why would he not want to remember her?

They clearly loved each other very much. They had a child together. That was his *family.*

"What happened to them?"

"Fuck, Eva!" He shoves a hand angrily through his hair and rubs the back of his neck. "You fucking want the truth?"

I nod as I watch the turmoil rising to a boiling point inside him.

He steps into me, stopping only a hairsbreadth from his chest hitting mine. "I fucking killed them."

13

ELIJAH

Eva recoils, her hazel eyes widen, and her lips part in a silent gasp. It's exactly the reaction I had hoped for.

It was a warning. One I hope she heeds.

She needs to stay far away from me. As far away as possible, even while she's sleeping in my bed, in my room, in this warehouse that has become my home since my release from prison. She needs to protect herself from me, from what I'm capable of.

"No." She shakes her head and wraps her trembling hands around her tiny waist. "You're lying."

I step into her until I can feel the intense, frightened energy radiating off her. My chest brushes against hers, and I suck in a breath, towering over her intentionally, accentuating our size difference so she'll finally feel the fear she should have if she had any self-preservation instinct.

"I'm *not* the good guy, Eva. Not by a fucking long shot."

Her bottom lip quivers. "I don't believe that."

I grab her biceps, digging my fingers into her soft flesh. "I'm not a good guy who has done some bad things. I'm a bad guy who did a good thing in helping you. That's it. You need to *stop* looking at me like I'm some sort of white-knight savior. You need to stop looking at me like *that*." I release one arm and point a finger in her face.

Her dark eyebrows rise, but her eyes never leave mine. "Like what?"

Like fucking what?

She has to know. She has to understand what she's doing to me.

I clench my jaw and squeeze her arm harder. "Like you want to fucking *kiss* me." The words come out on a growl, one so deep and menacing, any rational person would piss themselves and flee as fast as their legs could carry them.

But not Eva.

Of course, not fucking Eva.

The beautiful, sweet, innocent girl who has been through literal Hell doesn't have a fucking ounce of understanding about what she's getting herself into or asking for.

She doesn't back away from my harsh words. She just stands, staring at me with the same admiration she's had since I rescued her, only the healthy dose of fear that has always mixed with it seems to have dissipated.

"Goddammit, Eva." I release her arm and drop back from her.

"Why is it so wrong if I feel something for you?" Her question is so innocent, so honest, so completely her.

I growl and drag my hands through my hair as I pace away from her. "Because this," I motion between us, "can't happen. Even if I wanted it to."

Shit.

Those last few words weren't meant to be spoken out loud.

She takes a tiny step toward me. "Do you want it to?"

"Jesus Christ. Don't fucking ask me that." I drop my forehead against the wall, giving her my back.

She follows me across the room toward the window. "Why not? I've been here for a week, and I was afraid at first, but I think I've figured out what's going on, at least somewhat. And even knowing what I do, I still feel something for you that I have never felt for anyone before...*ever*."

Her last word is barely a whisper, but it sends goose bumps exploding across my skin. My heart races, and I struggle to suck in a deep breath.

She feels something.

"Of course, you do, Eva. You've got me lofted in your head in some sort of savior fairy tale. But I don't deserve it. Not any of it. Doing one good thing in your life does *not* eliminate all the bad ones."

"Including killing your wife and unborn child?"

A knife slices through my chest and twists into my heart. I force myself to drag my head up and meet her eyes. "Yes." I grit the word out between clenched teeth, but her soft eyes remain focused on me.

"I. Don't. Believe. You." She points toward the door. "If I go out there and ask any one of those people what happened, are they going to tell me that's what you did?"

Fuck.

No one here is stupid enough to talk about my past without my permission, but if she confronts them with that question, none of them are going to let her believe what they think is a lie but I know to be the truth.

"I did kill them."

I drop down onto the bed, rest my elbows on my knees, and scrub my hands over my face. Memories I've fought for a decade come flooding back in crystal clear clarity.

The sunny, cloudless sky of that summer day.

The light breeze that floated in through the open car windows.

The tinkle of laughter that slipped from between Claire's lips when the baby kicked.

The roar of the engine.

The squeal of tires.

The gunshots echoing in my ears.

The scream that ripped my heart from my chest.

Tears flow down my face, and I keep it covered. I can't look at Eva knowing what I did...what I caused... "I set it in motion. They died because of me. It's on *me*."

No amount of penance or self-flagellation will ever be enough to punish me for what I did. Every day I sat in that ten-by-ten cell, I relived that day second by second, wondering what I could have done differently, how I could have changed things. Every moment I was in that physical prison, I was in another of my own making—breathing when they weren't. Living when they were gone.

I don't deserve to be here. I don't deserve to see the sun rise and set every day when they're gone.

A sob threatens to rip from my chest, but a small, warm hand on the back of my neck makes me jerk up my head. Eva stands at my side, staring down at me with compassion I don't deserve wetting her eyes. I can't look at her. I bury my face in my hands again, and she drops to her knees and wraps her small arms around me.

It's been ten damn years since I felt someone else's hands on me that weren't threatening. My body stiffens, and I almost throw her off. But despite all the reasons it shouldn't, her warm embrace momentarily lifts the cloud of darkness surrounding me, and for a brief second, I relax and breathe without the weight of the last decade on my chest.

No.

I can't allow myself to do this. I can't let this poor girl believe I'm someone or something I'm not. I can't let her carry any of my burden.

She's been through enough. She doesn't need me dragging her down further.

I force my head up and shake her arms from around me. "You need to leave. As soon as you're well enough and Preacher has everything arranged. You need to get as far away from me and all of this as possible."

Somewhere safe where even I can't find you.

Eva leans in and presses her forehead against mine. "You don't want me to leave."

Shit.

"Claire died because she trusted me and believed I would keep her safe."

"Tell me what happened." Her request is quiet and reverent.

And I'm *this* damn close to revealing every sordid detail. The only thing stopping me is the selfish desire to see the adoration in her gaze one last time. It will be gone the second she learns what I did.

I pull back and capture her face between my palms. Her bronze skin practically glows in the moonlight streaming in from the window, and her tongue darts out and across her lips, wetting them and drawing me forward like a towline until our breaths mingle.

Fuck it.

I press my lips to hers softly, giving her and myself every chance to stop the insanity easily, but neither of us does. Instead, she pushes into me, kissing me harder, deeper, and wraps her arms around my neck to pull me even closer. My hands find her hips, and I drag her between my knees, angling her face up to mine to get her exactly where I want her and deepen our kiss even more.

This is wrong. So damn wrong on so many fucking levels.

Eva has been through unimaginable torture and pain and deserves so much better than a broken, incomplete asshole like me. Yet I can't push her away. I can't break off this very real connection I haven't felt with another person in a decade.

I'm a selfish bastard, and she's going to be the one who pays the price for it in the end. She's too young and goddamn sweet to understand why this is so dangerous. Why *I* am so damn dangerous.

But she'll learn soon enough. And then, she'll be gone. Off to her new life. One far away from this mess and her past.

I only hope she can outrun hers like she so desperately wants to. God fucking knows I've tried and have only managed to run head-long into it again.

Her fingers curl into the back of my neck, and I slide my tongue along the seam of her lips. She opens for me, and a tiny mewl slips from her.

The sound morphs in my head into a baby's cry.

No.

I jerk back and push her away.

She rocks backward on her knees, and her eyes fly open. Her brow furrows, and she reaches out for me. "What's wrong?"

I bat her hand away and shove to my feet to put some much-needed distance between us. My hands hit the wall, and I drop my head between my arms. "Stop. That was a mistake."

One that won't happen again.

The sound of Eva rising to her feet doesn't make me turn back to her. If I do, if I see the hurt on her face, in her kind eyes, it might completely break me.

"Elijah, please..."

There's absolutely nothing she can say that will change anything about this moment or the fact that the kiss we just shared was wrong and will never happen again.

I whirl around to tell her just that, but the shrill ring of the burner phone in my pocket stops me before I can utter a single word.

Only one person has this number.

Erjon.

That was much faster than I expected. Although, walking in and sitting down in the club was like rubbing myself right in his face. He probably wants to know what I want.

I hold up a hand to silence Eva and swipe to accept the call from an unknown number. My hands shake, though I don't know whether it's from what just happened with Evangeline or because of who will be on the other end of the line. "Hello?"

"Mr. Swift...I heard you were looking to speak to me."

No intro. No confirmation of who he is. Nothing.

An ice-cold chill rolls over my skin, and I shudder. I may not have ever met Erjon, but I know his type. I know *their* type. I know what they're capable of and have experienced it first-hand. So has Evangeline and all the other women on that ship.

I clear my throat. "Yes. I would love the opportunity to speak with you about a potential working relationship."

He chuckles. "That's quite surprising, Mr. Swift. Given the circumstances."

The man has every right to be suspicious, but I need to push my true feelings about him aside if I'm going to get the information we need.

"I had a lot of time to think about what happened while I was in prison. My feelings have changed."

Silence fills the line, and I pull the phone back from my ear to check to make sure the call is still connected. He's there. The asshole just isn't saying anything.

Finally, he sighs. "This isn't a conversation we should be having over the phone, Mr. Swift. You know where to find me."

Click.

The line goes dead.

"Who was that?"

I glance up at Eva. The concern in her gaze squeezes like a vise around my chest. "No one you need to worry about."

The corners of her kiss-swollen lips turn down into a tiny frown. "Then why do you look like you've seen a ghost. You're shaking."

Shit.

All those years I spent in a cell, I learned to conceal my feelings, to hold them in and lock them away so no one would see any of my weaknesses and try to exploit them. I was a rock. A stone-cold prisoner who didn't talk to anyone and didn't show an ounce of emotion. And since my release, I've done everything in my power to stay that way. But being on the outside makes it a thousand times harder.

I have to witness everyone else living. Finding love. Having babies. Getting what they've always wanted. I fucking had it, and I threw it all away with my selfishness. I *let it* be taken from me.

And ever since I saw Eva on that ship, the cold, harsh reality of that has been slapping me in the face every single time I look at her.

Knowing I'm about to face down the men who kidnapped her has eliminated any ability I had left to rein myself in.

She deserves to know the truth. So she can have some peace of mind.

"That was the head of the group that kidnapped you."

"What? Why is he calling you?"

I rub at my jaw. "Because I went looking for him. To get information on the current state of the organization. So we know we've taken care of anyone involved when this is all done and over with."

Her bottom lip quivers. "Taken care of?"

Despite knowing how dangerous it is to be close to her, I take two steps and reach out to grab her chin and tilt her face up to mine. "No one will ever hurt you again. I promise you that. We're going to kill them all."

14

EVANGELINE

"*We're going to kill them all.*"

Elijah's words from last night should have terrified me. I should want out of here more than ever because even though the thought of all those monsters paying for what they did to all of us should be comforting, it only confirms what I've suspected. The men I'm here with are killers.

"I'm a bad guy who did a good thing in helping you. That's it."

They *are* bad guys. The worst kind. The most dangerous ones. The ones who can pass as good.

The men who took me are evil to their cores. There's nothing redeeming about them, nothing that might, even momentarily, confuse you into thinking they might have a heart.

But these guys, Elijah's crew, they're different. They're bad to the bone, but somewhere deep in the marrow, there's a flicker of human decency. There's a little something that keeps them from becoming mindless killing machines. I won't go so far as to call it a conscience. I'm not *that* naïve to believe they have them, but *something* made Elijah help me. Something made Rion agree to treat me and Preacher offer to assist me in creating a new life. Warwick seems to be their leader, and for him to be allowing all of this, and for a woman like Grace to be involved with him, he can't be all bad, either.

Cutter might be the only exception. The scarred man terrifies me almost as much as the men who took me.

So...I should be afraid. Yet, instead of being scared, instead of lying awake last night worrying about being here with them, I slept peacefully, like a baby, for the first time since this whole ordeal started.

I have no idea where Elijah slept, though. It certainly wasn't in his usual spot in the chair across the room. After his phone call and the promise he made me, he disappeared faster than smoke on the water and left me wondering where all of this is going to end.

If it ever is.

One thing is clear, though. They're planning something very dangerous. They're going into enemy territory without important information. Information that will help keep them safe and could save other lives. Information I have.

It's been bouncing around in my head ever since I got here, and the endless debate with myself about how much to tell them and whether I can really trust them or not has been relentless. But after what happened last night between Elijah and me, the answer is finally clear.

I need to help them any way I can.

Not only to make sure the men who did this pay but also to ensure that the man who rescued me doesn't get hurt in the process.

If something happened to Elijah...especially when I could have done something to prevent it, I couldn't live with myself.

I pull open the door to Elijah's room and step out into the hallway. Other than using the bathroom and eating the few meals that weren't brought to me, I haven't left this room the entire time I've been here.

That changes now.

Hiding in here, waiting for my new life to be handed to me, isn't an option anymore. I need to step up and help make it happen.

I square my shoulders and move down the hallway toward the voices. My bare feet barely make a sound on the cold concrete floors. All five of them and Valentina sit around the massive wooden table, deep in discussion about something that has everyone looking tense.

Bile rises in my throat.

You can do this, Eva.

No one notices me. That seems to be the story of my life.

And as soon as someone did, I ended up chained in the hold of a ship to be sold off as a sex slave.

I clear my throat. The conversation ceases, and all eyes turn to me where I stand at the end of the hallway.

Elijah pushes up from his chair and approaches me slowly. "Eva, are you okay?"

I nod and glance behind him at the others. Valentina watches me expectantly. She's the only one of the girls at the table, and given what I've managed to learn, it makes sense. She seems to be just as powerful, if not more so, than these guys. Yet, there's something deeply kind and caring in her eyes. She's not completely hardened like them.

"I need to tell you something."

Elijah's brow furrows, and he takes another step toward me. "What is it?"

"I need to talk to all of you."

His eyebrows fly up, and he searches my face. He probably thought it had something to do with what happened between us last night, and while that may have been the catalyst for finally coming forward and telling him what I know, it ultimately has nothing to do with our kiss and everything to do with my wanting to give them the best chance possible to destroy those bastards.

He motions for me to follow him over to the table and pulls out an empty chair next to him for me to sit. I look around at all the expectant faces as they wait for me to say something. Valentina offers me a kind smile, and I manage to swallow through the lump in my throat.

"I have some information that may be useful to you."

All eyes remain locked on me. Even the ones I can't see, hidden behind the reflective aviator glasses Cutter wears, assess me, stripping me bare of any ability to hide.

Warwick nods. "Information about what?"

I consider my words for a moment as nerves suddenly cause my stomach to churn. They won't believe me.

How do I explain in it in a way they'll understand?

It's probably best to just be direct. "The Albanians and their operation."

Rion chuckles and leans back in his chair with his arms crossed over his chest. "Well, I'll be damned."

Cutter scowls at me from across the table but otherwise doesn't react. Milo continues to snooze on his lap, and Cutter's hand rests motionless on Milo's back.

Warwick leans forward to rest his elbows on the table. "What sort of information?"

What he really means is what could I possibly know that they have no idea about.

I take a deep breath and clasp my hands together on my lap. The last thing I want to do is relive any of the time I spent on that ship or bring up any of the memories of anything that happened there, but I need to. To help them. Ultimately, to help myself. "You're right that the men who took me are Albanian. From Chicago. At least, that's where were headed."

Warwick nods. "We knew that." He glances at Valentina.

"Valentina has connections in Chicago to keep her abreast of a lot of what happens there."

I nod. "I overheard things."

Warwick's eyes widen.

Cutter leans forward. "What sort of things?" His voice is low, almost a growl, and it causes goose bumps to roll across my skin. Milo doesn't even react—apparently used to his owner's attitude.

I swallow thickly and shrug, trying my best to keep my spine straight and my shoulders set. I don't want him to see my nerves. "A lot of things. Several of the men weren't very good about paying attention to who was around and might be listening when they talked. They probably assumed we were too weak to notice or care what they were saying or that we wouldn't understand them."

Warwick raises an eyebrow. "But, you could understand them?"

I nod slowly. "Sometimes they spoke Albanian, and by the end, I understood some of it, but they often spoke English because several of the guys were American born and they didn't understand Albanian enough to carry on a conversation."

Cutter grunts and leans back in his chair. "Sounds rather convenient."

Elijah slams his hand on the table. "What the fuck is that supposed to mean?"

I glance at him out of the corner of my eye. His clenched jaw. The vein throbbing at his temple. He's ready to launch himself across the table at Cutter.

For me.

And Cutter doesn't give a shit.

He shrugs. "Just that it seems awfully convenient that she's been here for a week and hasn't said a word, yet now, she suddenly decides to come forward with this information she supposedly overheard right at the same time we are getting ready to infiltrate their organization. I don't trust it." He growls. "I don't trust *her*."

Valentina reaches over and smacks Cutter's shoulder. "*Vai all'inferno*." She smiles at me and leans closer. "What were you able to learn?"

I open my mouth, but nothing comes out. Having everyone at the table watching me has stolen my ability to speak.

Rion pushes back from the table and climbs to his feet. "I'll be right back." He disappears through the kitchen door.

Elijah places a hand on my shoulder as he leans in. "Don't pay any attention to Cutter."

I force a smile and nod. It's hard to ignore the man when he's sitting only a few feet away from me with such palpable disdain and mistrust.

Rion returns with a beer in one hand and a bottle of water in the other. He hands me the water.

"Thank you."

He nods before he drops back into his chair and takes a long swig of the beer.

It's a little early to be drinking, but who am I to judge? These guys have likely seen and done things in their lives I can't even fathom. How they choose to deal with it is none of my business.

I twist off the cap and take two long pulls of the cold water. Everyone watches me intently, and the moment I set the bottle on the table, the pressure to continue with what I know practically crushes me.

"I don't want to know the details, but I know what you intend to do. I thought it would be helpful to confirm that a man named Erjon is their leader. He took over when the previous head of the family died. I didn't quite understand all of it when they were talking. Apparently, Erjon had been working on establishing the human trafficking ring for a while, though, because the guys who took me said they made their first run through Central Europe and the South Pacific within weeks of Erjon taking power."

Valentina smacks the table. "I knew it. I knew Aleksander couldn't have been involved in this. It was Erjon."

Warwick glances at her before returning his attention to me. "What else did you learn that might be helpful?"

I suck in a deep breath and squeeze my eyes shut. "One of the crewmen talked to me. A lot." I breathe slowly, in and out, trying to rid myself of the smell he always brought with him, the one I can't forget. "He told me they made a trip every six weeks or so, on a constant schedule. But…"

My hand shakes as I reach out for the water bottle. I take another drink and clench the plastic in my hand.

"They were able to get hold of something that needs to get here fast. They couldn't get it on board with us, so there's another shipment coming right behind us. I think he said it would arrive a week or so after our ship. Maybe it's an opportunity for you to take out some of the crew when they don't have Erjon's protection."

"Shit." Warwick shoves a hand through his hair. "When?"

"How long have I been here?" I don't even know. Between my illness and the fact that I haven't been watching the news or on any social media, I've lost all concept of time.

Elijah raps his knuckles against the table. "Seven days, three hours, and forty-five minutes."

All heads turn toward him.

"Fuck." Cutter pushes away from the table, sets a startled Milo to the floor, and rises to his feet. His palms press flat on the wooden surface separating us, and he leans across it toward me. "That means we basically have no time to track down that ship and intercept it. Even if it hasn't already made it to Chicago, we have no time to plan a raid. This time, they'll be ready for us. And you didn't fucking think to mention this until *now*?"

Elijah jumps up and slams his fist against the table. "Fuck you, Cutter. Leave her alone."

"Why should I?" Cutter rises to his full height. "She's a fucking liability, and now, we find out she's been hiding this from us? You should have let her die on that fucking ship."

Everyone at the table seems to freeze. Everyone except Elijah. He's around the table and throwing a punch at Cutter so fast, no one has time to intercept him.

Cutter's left arm flies up to deflect the blow, and his right fist connects with Elijah's jaw.

Rion is on his feet and dragging Cutter back before Warwick can even get out of his chair.

The leader of this ragtag group pushes against Elijah's chest, putting several feet between him and Cutter, who still pulls against Rion's hold. If Rion wasn't quite possibly the largest man I've ever seen in my life, I doubt he could have held Cutter back.

Elijah seethes and resists Warwick's attempt to move him even farther back. "Don't you ever fucking talk about her like that. She's the *victim* here, Cutter. Try to remember that."

Cutter shakes his head. "You're so fucking blind to what's happening here, E."

"Oh, really? Like you were when Valentina came in here and used you to get to Arturo and step up as head of the family?"

Oh shit.

I have no idea what the hell they're talking about, but Valentina's entire body stiffens, and a dark cloud seems to settle over Cutter.

Warwick shoves E back toward the hallway to the bedrooms. "Get the fuck out of here before Cutter kills you, E. Cool the fuck off." Warwick whirls around and points at Cutter.

"And you...keep your fucking mouth shut. I swear to God, if you start shit now, with Grace pregnant and about to give birth and the FBI potentially with information that can ID us, I cannot guarantee you'll walk out of here alive."

Holy shit.

Rion releases Cutter, who clenches his jaw and storms off and out of the warehouse without a glance back. Milo rushes after him but has the door slammed in his face. He stares at it for a moment before turning around and trudging slowly back toward the rest of us. E disappears down the hallway toward his room.

And I'm left sitting speechless at the table with Valentina, Rion, Warwick, and Preacher, who hasn't said a word since I came out here.

He clears his throat and rubs a hand over his beard. "And you fuckers wonder why I never leave my room and prefer the company of computers." He pushes to his feet and offers me a sympathetic smile. "You didn't do anything wrong, Eva. Come tell me every detail you can remember, and I'll start tracking down the next ship and getting what we need to make a plan."

Valentina releases a deep sigh. "What about Erjon? He told E to come to him. Should we leave him waiting?"

Warwick drops his head and clutches his hands behind his head. "What a fucking mess. We don't have time to plan a raid on this next shipment and take care of Erjon and his Chicago crew before we would need to hit the water. He'll have to wait. The women who are on that ship can't."

Tears sting my eyes. Maybe these guys are more human than I gave them credit for.

Except for Cutter.

Those glasses have blinded him to what's really going on here. I'm trying to help them, not harm them. I only hope he can see the truth.

15

ELIJAH

"I don't like this."

We all glance at Cutter. It's at least the sixth time he's said that since our conversation with Eva last night.

Warwick scoffs at him. "When was the last time you liked anything?"

Rion snorts and shakes his head. "He sure likes being buried balls deep in Valentina."

Cutter smacks the back of Rion's head. "You're lucky we're about to go take out these assholes, or you'd be the one in the sights of my 1911."

I grit my teeth together and tighten my hand around my gun. This is always the worst part—sitting here, waiting to strike—and listening to these guys joke around when innocent lives hang in the balance is making my trigger finger twitchy.

As much as I hate Cutter for what he said the other night about Eva, I have to fucking agree with him now. I don't like this at all. Not one fucking bit. By the time Eva gave Preacher the little information she had about the ship and shipment and he tracked it down, it was far too late for us to intercept them in the water.

Which brought us here, to the port in Chicago, waiting for the ship to dock and for these bastards to make an appearance so we can annihilate them and rescue the girls.

It's less than ideal.

Out on the water, no one's watching. The only eyes out there are the Coast Guard, and what they're capable of monitoring is a fucking joke. Lake Michigan alone covers 22,000 square miles, and if you throw in the rest of the Great Lakes, there are almost 95,000 square miles of water. When we raid a ship, we get on, get what we need, and are gone before they ever even know anything is wrong.

But here...I survey the area again. We're surrounded by a thousand different ways this could go wrong.

Dock security. A passerby seeing or overhearing something. A cop happening to drive by on his route.

It's the kind of position we never want to find ourselves in. And Cutter isn't letting go of the fact that Eva could've told us earlier.

If we weren't about to risk our fucking lives right now to intercept this shipment of women, he and I might be coming to blows...after he gets done with Rion for that comment about Valentina.

They're both assholes.

It's not fair to be taking it out on Eva. She had every right to question our motives and be reluctant to share anything with us. If Cutter keeps up this attack on her, we're going to have a very serious issue. Everyone knows it, too. The way War and Rion put themselves between us tonight proves it. The last thing we need is tension in our own ranks when we're about to do this take-down very publicly.

Warwick checks his watch. "They should be pulling in soon. Any minute now."

Preacher's been monitoring them, and it makes sense they come in this time of night when the docks are quiet and empty.

Especially if they're unloading the type of cargo that we think they are.

No sooner have the words left War's mouth than Cutter points toward the end of the dock. A green-hulled ship inches in slowly. *The Emerald Lady*. Exactly what we've been waiting for.

And where we wait behind a set of railcars along the train tracks that cut through the port gives us the perfect line of sight to where they will offload.

Someone throws a line over the side and jumps from the deck to tie up the ship. Men hustle back and forth along the deck, yelling, but we're too far away for me to make out anything they're saying.

Warwick nods at each of us. "We wait until their transportation shows up and they start unloading."

No shit.

He doesn't need to tell us the plan again. This may be a rush job, but Cutter made it very clear what we were supposed to do. Any chance to eliminate some additional guys involved in this is too important to pass up. If we wait for their drivers, we should get several more of these fuckers.

We hunker down and watch through our NODS night vision glasses as the men jump down onto the dock. Any other ship would have to send its cargo through customs, but these guys have a system. One that makes this pretty damn easy for them by simply paying off dock security and a few workers to turn a blind eye when they come in. There isn't a single soul in sight. They will just unload and disappear into the night before anyone even knows they were here...

And leave a trail of destroyed lives in their wake. Innocent women and girls like Eva, who will never be the same and who can never go back to their old lives.

War nudges me in the arm and nods toward a line of three

white conversion vans with blacked-out windows pulling in. "That must be their transportation."

My chest tightens. This is our chance to eliminate a huge part of their operation. Combined with the men we killed on the *Wanderer* when we rescued the girls, this will be a major blow—one that will hopefully set it up for us to finally take Erjon and his crew down for good.

Two more men climb down from the ship and make their way over to the vans. The three drivers climb out and greet the guys from the ship with half-hugs and back slaps. The seven of them stand around, laughing and smoking like they don't have a fucking care in the world.

Laugh all you want, assholes. That's the last smoke you're ever gonna have.

If they can be so cold and heartless when women are in the hold of that ship suffering, when they know what's going to happen to those women is unthinkable, then they don't deserve to live.

Cutter motions for us to move.

It's time.

He raises his sniper rifle and takes out two before the men even realize what's happening. The remaining guys scramble to dive behind the vans and scream at each other in Albanian.

We move out from behind the railcar like a well-oiled machine and fire on the five remaining men. The barrage of bullets rains down on them and ping off the vans where they take cover.

One of the guys peeks his head over the hood of the front van, and Rion drops to his knees and fires under the chassis. Another scream rips through the night air. He hit him, but there's no way to tell how many of them are down.

Come out, come out, wherever you are, motherfuckers.

Another guy peeks around the corner of the back vehicle to our left, and I move off toward him, firing until I have to reload.

The split-second that takes me is one too many. He fires, and a bullet grazes my shoulder.

"Fuck."

It doesn't slow me down at all.

I charge forward, unleashing a firestorm on him as Rion, War, and Cutter do their best to eliminate the remaining men to my right. I duck behind a large stack of pallets for cover and peek around at the man who has somehow managed to avoid every one of my shots.

He's reloading. Time to fucking end this. I race forward and fire at him. My first shot hits his arm, and the weapon falls from his hand and skitters across the pavement.

I fire off three more shots into his chest.

"E! Let's go!"

I turn toward War's voice. Cutter and Rion approach the ship, and War stands, waiting for me. I grab the gun off the pavement and race to catch up with them. We don't have a lot of time. Someone will have heard those shots.

We climb aboard and split off—me behind Warwick and Rion with Cutter. They head for the stern of the ship while we make our way toward the wheelhouse near the bow. The vessel rolls in the water, the familiar creak of the tied lines in the metal rungs of the dock the only sound breaking the silence of the night.

It's too quiet.

Unease creeps across my skin while I stand watch as Warwick moves into the wheelhouse and clears it. No sign of any additional crew. We check the entire forward section of the ship then make our way toward the stern where the entry to the cargo hold lies.

The women will be down there. Probably cold, starved, sick, and terrified—just like Eva was.

Rion climbs from the cargo hold.

The hard set of his jaw slows my approach. "How many are there?"

He sighs and rubs the back of his neck. "Zero."

Warwick and I freeze, and I shake my head.

I must've misheard him.

"What do you mean, zero?"

He shrugs, and Cutter appears behind him.

Rion shakes his head. "There's no one down there. No additional crew. No women."

What the hell?

I storm over the hold and glance down. "Where the fuck are they?"

Cutter nods toward the hold. "They have a whole fuckload of guns down there. I broke open one of the pallets."

White-hot rage floods my veins. "So, where the hell are the women being held?"

He shrugs. "Not fucking here, apparently."

I squeeze my hand around my gun and turn back toward where we climbed on board.

War grabs my arm. "Where the fuck are you going?"

"To get some fucking answers." I shake off his hold and jump from the ship down to the dock.

There's no way Eva sent us on a wild goose chase. Those women are somewhere, and I need to find them. These guys could have made a stop we're not aware of on the way here and unloaded them, or there could be a second boat waiting to come in. One of these fuckers has to know.

I make my way over to the men laid out on the pavement around the vans. Blood pools under most of them, and I quickly check them one by one.

"What the hell are you doing?" Warwick stops at my side.

"Looking for somebody who is still breathing who can answer some fucking questions."

He waves a hand. "They all look dead to me."

Fucking hell.

They should all be dead if we were all doing our jobs right. No one to give me the answers we need.

A gurgling moan comes from the other side of one of the vans, and I push to my feet. I wander around to the other side of the van and freeze. It's the man I shot before we boarded.

Warwick points. "What the fuck was that?"

Shit.

I squat next to the man and watch his chest rise and fall erratically. Gurgling sounds emanate from his throat. Any other time, it would be a massive mistake not to make sure he was dead before I followed the guys on board, one I would be beating myself up over and getting reamed out for by Cutter and everyone else.

But now, it definitely plays in our favor.

Maybe I can get some fucking answers.

"Jesus Christ." Cutter comes to a stop next to me. "You didn't make sure he was dead?"

"Don't fucking start with me right now, Cutter."

"Kill him. We need to get the fuck out of here."

Warwick pushes against Cutter's chest, backing him away, then glances over his shoulder to me. "Cutter's right. We need to get the fuck out of here. That amount of gunfire is going to draw attention very quickly."

Cutter snarls. "Finish him. We don't have time for this."

I shake my head and focus on the bleeding man at my feet. "Not until I find out where the women are." I lean over him and press my hand over the wound in his chest, digging my palm into it.

Hope that hurts like a bitch.

He screams and thrashes beneath me, and his eyes fly open. "Where are the women?"

His gaze shoots all around him before it finally comes to me. "Fuck you."

My fist connects with his face, and the sound of his nose shattering fills the night. Blood gushes out of his mouth and nostrils, and I wrap my now bloody hand around his throat.

"Tell me where the fuck the shipment of women is. Did you drop them off somewhere else already?"

He gurgles, and I twist the fingers of my other hand into the wound on his chest. Another scream cuts through the air, muffled by the way I'm restricting his breathing.

"Where are they?"

The man grits his teeth and groans. His ghostly-white pallor means he's close to death. "There aren't any. Only guns this time."

This time.

"When's the next shipment scheduled?"

He shakes his head, and I twist my fingers.

Another garbled scream works from his mouth. "A month from now. But they've already left."

Shit.

"Where are they coming from?"

A sneer twists his bloody lips. "I'll die before I fucking tell you anything else."

"That can definitely be arranged. Now, do you want to go quickly, or do you want me to drag this out?"

He coughs up a river of blood and turns his head to the side. "You will never stop it. You'll never stop us. We—"

A bullet to the center of his forehead silences him. Blood sprays back on me, and I jerk and stare up at Cutter, his arm extended and his gun pointed right at the man.

Cutter's scarred lips curl into a wicked grin. "Sleep tight, motherfucker."

"Why the fuck did you do that?" I wasn't done questioning him. I could have gotten us more information.

"Because you wouldn't. We need to get the fuck out of here.

He's not gonna give you anything that we can't find out another way. Let's go."

I surge to my feet and charge at him, but Rion grabs me around the shoulders and pulls me back, sending pain lacing through my arm.

"Relax, E. You two can duke it out later." He shoves me in the direction of where the SUV is hidden along the side of the railyard.

I want nothing more than to give Cutter exactly what I handed to the dead asshole on the ground, but there's no time now. Not if we want to get out of here clean.

We take off at a sprint. My anger tightens every muscle of my body.

This whole fucking thing was for nothing.

Or maybe not nothing.

Those guns won't get to the Albanians, so that's a good thing. But there's still another shipment of women out there, other innocent girls who were ripped from their lives and their families.

Somebody has to pay for that.

I'll make sure of it.

16

EVANGELINE

"Why aren't they back yet?" I pace the length of Grace and Warwick's small bedroom for the thousandth time since the guys left and step out onto the landing of the large metal staircase that leads down to the warehouse floor.

Grace motions me back in and pats the side of the bed next to her on the side not occupied by a snoring Milo. "Like I've told you a hundred times, this is the worst part about this life. But if something were wrong, Preacher would've told us so we could be prepared."

He's already updated us on the fact that the women weren't on board as expected. Whether they changed their plans, or I misunderstood what the shipment was, guilt has weighed on me at the danger I put them in, essentially for nothing.

Yes, the weapons won't make it to the Albanians, and several members of Erjon's crew were taken out, but it means there could also be another shipment of women out there somewhere with no one to rescue them.

I take a deep breath and lower myself onto the bed next to her. "I can't believe you're so calm."

She rubs her large belly and chuckles. "I don't have any

other choice if I want to keep this little guy in for the next couple weeks."

It takes me a lot to force a smile. I can't imagine being pregnant and going through what she does every time these guys go out there. No one has offered me much information, but between overhearing a few conversations and the things people *have* told me, I think it's safe to say I know what these guys are...

Pirates.

Not the swashbuckling, sword-wielding ones I used to read about in old romance novels. These are the kind who carry guns and kill people. They were only on my ship because they wanted the cargo. It wasn't a rescue mission. They weren't there to help us. It was just the position they ended up in when they didn't find what they expected on board.

And now, because of me, they've been pulled into this massive human trafficking ring, and I'm still smack dab at the center of it.

Grace rubs my back softly. "Really, try not to worry. These guys are good at what they do and know how to take care of themselves."

"Shouldn't I be the one comforting you?"

She laughs and shakes her head. "I've been here long enough that I know what to expect. I'm definitely nervous; I'm just doing my best to not show it and trying to stay calm for the baby's sake."

Grace makes it seem so easy.

No amount of deep breathing and good thoughts will ease this tension coiling in my body.

Nothing will until Elijah steps safely through that door.

I shouldn't care this much. I shouldn't be worrying about a man I barely know, but the time we've spent together has bonded me to him in a way I can't explain. I owe him my *life,* and I can't stand the thought of anything bad happening to him.

Footsteps on the stairs make me pause. I leap off the bed and race to the door.

Preacher meets me at the top of the landing. "They'll be back any minute."

A huge breath rushes from my chest. "Oh, thank God."

He already told us they were on their way home, but the several hours it takes to get from Chicago back here feels like an eternity. I turn back to ensure Grace heard him.

Grace waves me away. "Go meet them down there, but honey..." She pauses and seems to consider her next words. "Just a warning. E isn't exactly someone you want to be around when he gets back from a mission."

"What does that mean?"

She sighs and shifts herself into a different position. "Cutter and Rion were trained for this, and Preacher saw a lot of it when he worked with the CIA and was embedded in war zones. Warwick," she releases a deep sigh, "he got himself involved. But E...he's got a soft spot the other guys don't. He's the one most affected by what they do. He might need some space."

Space. How do I give him space when I'm sleeping in his bed, in his room, in the only part of this warehouse that's really his?

I don't even know where he's been sleeping since he abandoned the chair in his room. Just anywhere away from me, apparently. That should be a sign to stay away, but I can't seem to.

The man continues to spin my world off its axis when it's already so off-balance. He's so hot and cold. Soft and hard. Angry and caring. It's like he can't decide who or what he wants to be.

And I can't seem to stay away, despite his warning.

I grip the doorjamb and stare at Grace. I've been waiting for someone to offer me some information about what happened to E and his family, and this might be my only opportunity. "Does this have anything to do with what happened to his wife and baby?"

Grace's smile falters, and she sucks in a deep breath. "I don't know what he told you, but it's not my place to tell you more if he doesn't want you to know."

Exactly what I thought her response would be.

I respect the way everyone here keeps each other's secrets, but it's still frustrating not to understand what's driving him. Maybe if I had an idea of why he's so fractured, I could figure out a way to help put him back together again.

"Thank you, Grace. For everything."

She smiles and waves me off again. I follow Preacher down the metal stairs, and my feet hit the concrete at the same time the door to the warehouse opens.

Warwick enters first and beelines straight for where I stand at the bottom of the steps.

I motion to the room behind me. "She's upstairs. She's fine."

He offers me a curt nod and races up the steps. Milo slowly makes his way down, no doubt looking for Cutter.

Cutter and Rion wander in next, carrying two large duffel bags. Both look exhausted but no worse for wear. Milo meets them halfway across the warehouse, and Cutter scoops him and whispers something to the dog.

The door opens a final time, and E steps through. My breath catches in my throat.

Oh, my God.

Blood covers his hands and soaks one sleeve of his dark-gray, long-sleeved T-shirt. Smears of deep crimson slash across his jawline and neck.

"Elijah!" His name echoes through the warehouse, and I rush across the concrete toward him.

His hooded gaze shifts up to meet mine, and his eyes widen just before I jolt to a stop in front of him.

I run my hand over his blood-soaked shirt. "Oh, my God. Are you okay?"

He shoves me away from him. "It's not my blood." He glances at his arm. "At least, most of it isn't."

Oh, thank God. It's not his...

Blood.

That's *a lot* of blood. Whomever it belongs to isn't breathing right now.

I should probably feel bad about that. Have some sort of guilt over the fact that I helped send these mercenaries out to kill, but the people they went after aren't anyone who deserves to live anyway. Not with what they do.

It isn't very Christian of me to wish death on others. The power of forgiveness was always stressed growing up. But it's how I feel, and there isn't anything I can do about that. Those men, or at least their partners, ripped me away from my life. From Ma and Pa. From my future. It's all gone now. And then they put me through weeks of torture because they're soulless bastards.

They deserved to pay for what they did. So rather than the weight of guilt sitting on my shoulders, it's only the concern for why Elijah's blue eyes look so empty. So lost. Why he looks so tense that he might snap at any moment.

He pushes past me without another look and storms down the hallway toward his room.

What just happened?

I turn to go after him and find Preacher standing halfway across the warehouse with his arms crossed over his chest, watching me. I approach him slowly, and his dark eyes soften.

"Don't go after him, Eva."

"Why not? He's hurt and clearly upset."

Preacher glances over his shoulder in the direction E just went and nods. "He is, but Rion will take care of whatever injury he might have, and E is pretty volatile when he's like this. You don't want to be anywhere near him right now."

I shouldn't want to be. That much is true. That we can *agree* on.

But my heart aches to follow that complicated, mysterious man down that hallway. My fingers itch to touch him and comfort him and give him whatever he needs in this moment. Of all the guys who make up this crew, Preacher seems the most thoughtful and genuine. If anyone will give me the truth, it's him.

I step closer and scan the warehouse to make sure no one is around. "Tell me what happened to Elijah's wife and baby."

"Fuck." He scrubs a hand across his short beard and glances at the ceiling. "I can't do that, Eva, but I will tell you that what we're doing right now with the Albanians is bringing up a lot of bad memories for him. Ones that would crush a man who isn't as strong as E."

Whatever happened was bad. Really bad. And he's suffering right now because of me, because he chose to help me, because he came into my life and saved it.

I can't let him suffer alone. No matter what it costs me.

I shift to move past Preacher, but he grabs me gently by the shoulder.

"Just be careful, Evangeline."

"I will be."

I pull away from him and walk slowly down the hallway. I've been careful my entire life. Always following the rules. Always at home before dark. Always to class on time. Never late for work. Straight home afterward. I led the safest life I possibly could, and yet, look at what that got me, where I ended up because of it. I ended up here because I thought I was safe.

My life has proven that there is no safe. There may never be again.

That means there's nothing left to fear if I ever want to live again.

I make my way past the closed door of Cutter's room. E's door stands ajar, and I push it open and step inside.

He stands in the center of the room, staring down at his blood-covered hands. The stillness of the room seems unnatural. He doesn't seem to notice me enter, and I approach him slowly, carefully so as not to startle him.

"Elijah?"

He doesn't move or acknowledge my presence.

I step around him and bend down to see his face.

Vacant eyes stare down, and tears trickle over his cheeks.

He's not in this room right now. He's somewhere else.

I touch his arm, and he jerks his head up, but his eyes don't focus on me.

"Claire?"

Oh, God. His wife.

Whatever happened out there tonight, it set off something inside him that sent him down a very dark path. I need to get him cleaned up. There's no way I can leave him like this.

I grab his arm. "Elijah, come with me."

The vacant look never leaves his eyes as I lead him down the hallway to the bathroom. I open the door and guide him in. The click of it closing into place behind us seems loud in the tiny, silent space, but he doesn't react; he just continues to focus on his bloody hands.

"Elijah, we need to get you out of these clothes."

No reaction.

I'm going to have to do this. He's not capable of taking care of himself right now. I grasp the hem of the shirt and tug it up. He raises his arms and lets me pull it over his head.

It falls to the cracked tile floor.

Blood trickles down his arm from a wound on his left bicep. That will have to be taken care of, but it doesn't look too bad. It's the least of my concerns. Whatever is going on in Elijah's head is burying him right now. I need to help dig him out.

I reach for the button of his jeans then jerk my hand away. I've never undressed a man before, and what I have to do sends heat rushing over my skin. Elijah is so beautiful—all hard, lean muscle and brilliant ink—but he's also broken.

This is definitely not how I imagined it going.

Blood smears across the denim have bile rising in my throat. I swallow through it, unbutton them, and pull down the zipper. E stares down—not watching what I'm doing but focused on some unknown spot in his mind. I tug down his jeans, keeping my gaze to the side.

Don't look down.

I keep my eyes averted and help him step out of the jeans. His legs shake, his entire body vibrating hard enough to make him stumble. I steady him with my hands. My chest aches watching him in so much pain, but I don't know what else I can do besides this. I rise to my feet, crank on the water in the shower, and stick my hand under the spray.

He stands catatonic in the center of the bathroom like I didn't just strip him bare. Like he isn't covered in blood and hurt.

Whatever is happening in his head needs to stop. I need to snap him out of it.

I grab his arm and lead him into the shower. He doesn't react to the hot spray hitting his skin.

"This will help, Elijah. Get cleaned up, and you'll feel better."

Hopefully.

I close the door to the shower and slip out of the bathroom as silently as I can. As much as my heart hurts to see him like this, I can't do anything else for him if he doesn't want my help.

With the door closed, I rest my palm against the door and

press my ear to the wood. The only sounds are the water and my own heartbeat thrumming in my ears.

Don't go in there, Eva. If he wanted you there, he would've asked you to stay.

Seconds tick by.

Minutes.

And still...no sound other than the water running.

I shouldn't but I can't stop myself from reaching out and grasping the door handle. It turns easily and silently, but even if it had made a noise, he wouldn't have heard it over the sound of the water pounding over him. I push it open slowly and step into the bathroom.

The warm, steamy air hits me, and I suck in a deep breath. My hand shakes as I reach behind me to shut the door.

His bloody clothes still lie in a pile on the floor, and billows of steam rise from above the shower door. The heavily fogged glass only permits me to see his ghostly outline, but Elijah stands under the hot spray with his hands pressed against the tile and his head dropped down between his shoulders.

He doesn't glance up as I approach. Doesn't move as I reach down and strip off my pants and underwear and the T-shirt that Grace gave me. He doesn't so much as flinch when I reach out and pull open the shower door and step inside.

What am I doing?

I don't have a clue. I should be terrified—of being naked with him. Of being so close to him when he's in this state. Of *him*.

Yet...I step forward and hesitantly lay my hand on his shoulder.

He flinches but doesn't say anything, and I gently run my fingers up and down his spine and step forward again until I can press my chest against his back and wrap my arms around him. His chest heaves, and he spins around, practically knocking me backward.

White-hot fire burns in his blue eyes rimmed in red. He clenches his jaw, and a muscle tics under the blood smear still covering the side of his face.

I let my eyes wander down to the bloodstains still marring his hands. Blood still seeps from a wound on his left bicep, down his forearm to drip into the water at our feet. I reach out, but he pulls back.

"What are you doing in here, Eva? You shouldn't be here."

No, I shouldn't. For a hundred different reasons.

"I...I don't have a clue why I'm here."

Not at all.

At first glance, this man is no different than the ones who took me. He's dangerous, volatile, and capable of killing someone with his bare hands. Yet, he's also damaged and clouded in the shroud of anguish that's so thick, I can barely see through it.

Barely, but I can.

There's more. Something underneath all that pain and anger. Something that draws me to him and makes it impossible to turn away.

I step into him and place my palms against his chest. "I'm here because you're upset, and you need me."

He stands stock-still for a second, glaring down at me with anger and something even more dangerous in his eyes, but then his shoulders slump, and his chest deflates. I step fully into his embrace and rest my cheek against his chest. His arms come up and wrap around me, and the hands covered in the blood of our mutual enemies press me even closer. I focus on the tile floor of the shower and watch the pink-tinged water swirling down the drain near our feet, taking with it any ability I may have ever had to say no to this man.

He's broken. Maybe beyond repair. But so am I.

I pull back from him and take one of his hands in mine. It shakes, and I clasp my fingers tightly around it and grasp the bar of soap. Each swipe helps to scrub away the remnants of whatever happened tonight.

Elijah stands motionless, letting me clean him up, and his breathing evens out. I switch to his other hand, then turn his arm to look at the wound there.

He tries to yank his hand from mine, but I clasp it even tighter.

"Let me help you, Elijah. The way you helped me."

17

ELIJAH

"Help me, Elijah. Help me!" She gasps, struggling to drag air into her lungs, desperate to take a single breath. "The baby!"

Her hands drop to her stomach, leaving bloody prints on the once-white T-shirt.

I press my hands against the wound in her chest and frantically search the car for anything I can use to help stop the bleeding. A towel? A shirt? Anything...

So much blood. So much fucking blood.

My vision blurs, and bile burns my throat. "It's okay, baby. You're gonna be all right."

Blood seeps from between my fingers and drips down to the upholstery of the car seat below her.

Everything is red. So fucking red.

This can't be happening. No. No. No. No. No. Not now.

I fumble for my cell phone in my back pocket and dial 9-1-1 with one slippery, bloody hand while trying to stem the flow of blood with the other. Her hands fall away from her belly, down into the pooling crimson on the seat.

"Nine. One. One. What is your emergency?"

My lungs burn. I can't seem to breathe in any air. "My wife... she's...she's been shot. There's so much blood. And she's pregnant..."

"Elijah." Eva's left hand brushes along my cheek, wiping away the blood smeared there. The blood of the man out on the pavement. "Elijah, stay with me."

With her.

Here.

I squeeze my eyes closed against the memories of the day I lost them.

The past. That was the past. Not today.

"Elijah." She captures my face between her palms and angles my head down. "Stay here."

My body trembles, and I shake my head.

I can't.

I hold up my hands.

Blood.

Even though she's washed them, blood still flows down them from that day. More blood than I had ever seen in my life. Too much.

"Elijah, tell me where you are. Tell me what happened."

"I..." My mouth opens and shuts, and I suck in a breath. "I did this."

It was me. Only me.

"You did what?"

Why can't she see it? Why can't she understand?

"I killed Claire and the baby."

"How? Elijah, tell me what happened."

The hot water beating down on us and Eva's soft touch are the only things keeping me from completely losing myself in the memory like I have so many times over the last decade. Completely drowning in the anguish and agony of what I did. Relieving every second over and over again.

Eva won't understand. She'll hate me if I tell her...

But maybe that's exactly what needs to happen to make her realize who I am.

She shouldn't be here. This shower. This bathroom. This warehouse. This city. This damn country. She should go home. Far away from me and this.

I squeeze my eyes closed. "It was just another deal. It was just like hundreds of others I had done. But I made a mistake." A massive one that cost Claire and our baby their lives. "I should never have betrayed them. But I didn't think I'd get caught. I never thought they would do something like this."

"You never thought who would do what?" Eva's voice is so soft, so even, like the words I just said didn't even faze her.

"I betrayed Saban."

"Who is Saban?"

This is where it comes—her anger. Her hate. It has to.

I force my eyes open to meet hers, to ensure she understands the truth. "He was the leader of the Albanian mob in Chicago back then."

Her tiny gasp brings me fully back to the present, and I stare down at her wide, startled eyes.

I scrub the water from my face. She knew I worked with the Albanians. I told her as much, but she could never have guessed the extent of what happened. "I was just a young, stupid kid who needed to make some money. Claire and I grew up in a city called Kenosha, which is halfway between Milwaukee and Chicago, right along a major drug route. Neither of us came from money. We were always struggling to make ends meet."

Claire's radiant smile fills my vision, and I blink it away. I won't be able to tell Eva what she needs to hear if all I see is that final smile she gave me before I got out of the car to run up to the porch of the house where I was conducting my sale. "We got married right after high school. Scraped and saved for our own apartment. I did what I had to, and often it was illegal. I started selling for them when she got pregnant. It was quick money, and I needed it."

My hands clench and open at my sides. Eva waits for me to continue, completely oblivious to the scalding water pouring over us.

"But I got greedy. I started cutting the product and selling the extra on the side. I never thought they'd find out. I never thought anything like this could happen."

I should have known, should have seen it coming.

She brushes her hand across my chest, and I close my eyes and absorb the feel of her touch on my skin.

Good. Real.

Nothing that I deserve.

Her fingers curl into my flesh. "They came after you?"

I open my eyes and shake my head, fighting the urge to wrap my arms around her. "No. They came after Claire."

Because of me. Because I put her in the crosshairs. Because they knew it was the way to truly hurt me and send a message to anyone else stupid enough to try anything or move against them. Because she *trusted* me.

Tears stream down Eva's face. She hasn't talked about her past, but it's clear she's never been exposed to anything like this before. The violence. The death. I never wanted to hurt Eva, but she needed to hear the truth. But seeing her reaction, the way her lips tremble and tears fall hurts more than I ever anticipated. "I told you I killed them."

"You didn't," she shakes her head, "you just made a bad decision."

No!

I push away from her until my back hits the tile wall, and I slide down onto my ass with my face in my hands. "It's my fault that Claire died in that car and our son was dead before they even got him out of her. I never even got to hold him."

A sob rips from somewhere deep in my chest, mirroring the

way my heart is shredding apart, thinking about what I lost. What I *did*.

The tears come hard and relentless, and I have zero power to stop them. A tidal wave of despair I usually manage to keep at bay around anyone else hits me so hard, it steals my breath and any ability to shake the memories from the forefront of my brain.

I'm lost to it.

Lost to the world.

Lost in the reality of what my life has become.

What *I* have become.

A shell of who I was.

Barely breathing and barely living.

Dragging myself through one second at a time until I can finally get what's coming to me in the fiery pits of Hell, though nothing can be as bad as living with the guilt and pain that's crashing over me, drowning me right now.

I gasp but can't find my breath. My entire body shakes, frozen and covered in goose bumps, even as hot water pelts my skin.

Darkness closes in around me, threatening to completely envelop me.

It's an old friend. One I usually welcome.

I've spent so much time there over the years, reliving every awful moment mixed in with all the good ones. Wondering what our son would have been like.

Would he have been blond like me or had dark, silky hair like Claire? Would he have had her quick smile and easy laugh or been more stoic like I am? Would he have loved chess or thought we were total nerds for playing all the time?

Images of the future that could have been mingled with what happened that day.

"No. No. No."

Small hands push my knees apart, and Eva shifts to kneel

between them. She knocks my hands from my face and takes it in her palms. Water still cascades around us, almost like a waterfall, capable of washing away the bloody evidence of tonight but not of what happened all those years ago.

That's a permanent stain that will never disappear, never even fade.

Eva brushes her thumb over my lips, stopping the word I said so many times that day and have repeated endlessly over the years. "What happened after that?"

I clench my jaw and squeeze my fists. The cool metal of the gun in my palm is as clear as it was that day. The weight of the weapon and the clear intent to kill with it.

The aftermath.

"The police questioned me. I made them believe it was a random drive-by. And then...I went to kill Saban."

Her arm trembles, and she pulls it away from my face. "Did you?"

She shouldn't want to touch me. Shouldn't want to be here with me...like this. Not when I'm a killer. Anyone with self-preservation instincts would run. When she hears it all, maybe she will get some sense of who and what I really am and want to leave.

"I went to kill the man responsible for Claire's death, and...I failed."

Miserable fucking failure.

"I tried to get to Saban, but he had too much security, too many men between him and me." I rest my arms on my knees and watch my hands shake as I mentally relive that day. "I killed one of them and shot two others before one of them shot me."

She reaches out slowly and runs her fingers over the scar on my left rib cage, where the bullet stopped me dead in my tracks.

"They would've killed me right then and there, but a police

car happened to be driving by Saban's headquarters and managed to stop them. Four of Saban's men died that day—the one I killed and three by the police."

Her fingers slowly trail down my side and come to a stop at my hip. "And you went to prison."

I nod slowly. "Then, I went to prison. The only reason I didn't end up with a much longer sentence was the amazing attorney my parents sold their house to pay for. He told the jury why I did it. He was going for jury nullification, and they acquitted me of everything but manslaughter, which has a much lower penalty range. The judge also felt for me, I think." I drop my head back against the tile and close my eyes, letting the scalding water beat down on my face and chest. "Everything that has happened in my life is my fault. I'm the only one to blame."

The only one who should bear the weight of this guilt.

Eva captures my face between her hands and drags it forward. Her lips brush over mine gently, slowly, almost reverently before she pulls away. "Everything you did in your life led you to be on that ship that day. If it weren't for you, I can't even think of where I'd be right now. Dead or in the hands of someone willing to do unspeakable things to me."

I let out a mirthless laugh that echoes off the tile and shake my head. "Instead, you're here with me. That's not much better."

She lets out an annoyed sigh. "You don't give yourself enough credit, Elijah."

"You give me too much, Evangeline." I swallow thickly. "The reason I went off on you about the chess pieces..." I shake my head. "I used to play with Claire. We were in the middle of a game when she died. I made my parents document exactly where the pieces were, and when I got released, I set it up exactly the same as it was that day. In the middle of a game that will never be finished. I flipped out on you over a damn game."

Her tears mix with the water pouring over us, and she doesn't say anything about my explanation.

No matter what she thinks, I'm a monster. One responsible for more deaths than I can even count at this point. I'm not someone she should be here with, let alone like this.

She's too kind. Too sweet. Too pure.

But as she shifts forward and climbs into my lap, wrapping her arms around me and burying her face against my neck, I do nothing to push her away.

18

EVANGELINE

I fell asleep in the arms of a broken man, and now, I'm waking to a cold, empty bed. The sheets beside me hold no lingering warmth from his body. He's been gone for a while.

Where is he?

I push myself up onto my elbows and scan the room—hoping deep in my heart that he'll be sitting in the chair he used to sleep in—but there's no sign of the man who fell apart in front of me, who ripped open his soul to let me see the deepest, darkest part of it, who let me see what carved him into who he is today.

Faint morning light peeks in from around the blinds covering the only window in the room.

It's morning, and I'm alone.

Just like I've been every morning since I got here except my first. I don't know why I thought this morning might be different, that things might have changed between us after what happened last night, after we held each other for hours, after his heartfelt confession, after the kiss we shared.

But apparently, it hasn't.

And I'm more confused than ever about what's happening

between us or how I'm supposed to feel, knowing the guys who rescued me also slaughtered so many people.

How did I end up here? Like this?

Just when I thought things couldn't get more complicated than they were when I was on that ship, Elijah Swift has to turn my entire world upside down yet again.

A light knock at the door has me jerking up and turning toward it. I glance down at Elijah's T-shirt that I slept in last night. It's probably a good thing he's not still here and in bed with me, otherwise whoever is at that door might get the wrong idea about what happened last night.

"Come in."

The door creaks open, and Everly sticks in her head. "I wasn't sure you were awake yet. I'm heading to the shop early today. I thought maybe you might want to get out of here and come with me."

"Am I allowed to do that?" I've been cooped up in this warehouse for so long, I assumed it was because they don't want me knowing where it is or running into anyone who might ask questions I don't have answers for.

Everly rolls her eyes and chuckles. "Of course, you're allowed to. You're not a prisoner here."

Sometimes it feels that way.

A prisoner in my own mind. A prisoner to what those men did. A prisoner to how I'm starting to feel about the man who rescued me.

Getting out of here may be just what I need to clear my head.

"I'd love to come."

Everly's lips tip into a smile. "Great. Do you need more clothes, or are you okay?"

I glance at the stack piled up on Elijah's dresser. "I'm okay. You girls have been more than generous. I can't thank you enough."

She waves me off dismissively. "You don't have to thank us. Get dressed and come out whenever you're ready. I'll wait in the kitchen, and you can grab a bite to eat before we go."

I want to ask her where Elijah is, but I bite my lip instead. "Okay, thanks."

She shuts the door, and I climb out of the warm, soft bed and into the chilly air and pad across the room to grab clothes to change into. By the time I pull open the door and make my way down to the kitchen, my stomach growls angrily.

I haven't had much of an appetite since I've been here—the lingering effects from whatever infection was raging through my body for so long—but now that I'm finally better, I feel like I could eat a horse.

Voices float out from the kitchen, and I enter slowly, holding my breath. I don't know what I'll say to Elijah this morning. His disappearing act seems to suggest he regrets opening up to me last night, but he clearly needed the catharsis. And now that I know the truth about what happened to Claire and their baby, I can so much better understand his agony and why he's in a downward spiral due to everything that's happened since they found me on that ship.

My gaze immediately covers the whole room, but there isn't any sign of Elijah.

Crap.

It's more disappointing than it should be, than I should *let* it be for my own mental health. Yet, I can't help but wonder where he disappeared to this morning.

Was he running from himself or from me?

Milo sleeps on the floor near where Everly leans back against the counter with a cup of coffee in her hand, and Grace perches precariously on a stool at the counter.

I thought she was supposed to stay in bed.

"You're up?"

She grins at me, and mischief dances in her green eye.

"Don't tell Warwick. I was going stir crazy up there, and the doctor did say it was okay for a few minutes."

A tray of blueberry muffins sits in the center of the counter. My stomach rumbles.

Grace nods toward it. "He made these this morning."

"Who?"

She chuckles. "E. He spends more time in this kitchen than anyone else. We would probably all starve without him."

"E can cook?"

Everly barks out a laugh. "He's an amazing cook. He learned while he was in prison."

A vague memory of someone telling me E was going to whip something up flits through my head, but I never really asked who made the things that have been set in front of me.

And he made my favorite muffins.

I mentioned it in passing over breakfast a few days ago. It wasn't a request, just part of the conversation going around the table.

He remembered. What does that mean?

As with everything related to E, I have a lot of questions and no answers.

I reach out and grab one, trying to appear as nonchalant as possible. "Where is he?"

They exchange a look and both grin at me.

Everly motions toward the lake. "He went for a run." She glances down at her watch. "Almost two hours ago. That's long, even for him."

"He has a lot on his mind." That's putting it mildly. There's no way I'll reveal what happened last night, though. I could never betray his trust like that.

I peel the paper off the muffin and sink my teeth into the sugar-encrusted top. The explosion of flavor on my tongue—sweet and bitter—and the juxtaposition of the soft and chewy texture make me moan. "Oh, my God, these are so good."

Tears prick my eyes, despite how much I desperately needed this stupid muffin. I'll never have Ma's muffins again. I'll never have any of those familiar flavors of her cooking, none of the family recipes.

It's almost enough to make me reconsider my stance on not going home, but there's no way. There are too many reasons I have to stay away.

Everly drains her mug. "Everything E makes is delicious. And something tells me he may have made those for someone specific." She winks at me. "You ready to go? You can eat that in my car."

"Yup." I barely manage to mumble the word around a mouthful and grab another one for the road.

Grace pushes to her feet and grabs her lower back. "I'm glad to see you up and around and feeling well enough to go out." She reaches out and rests her hand on my forearm. "You're gonna be okay, honey."

Her words bring back the sting of tears to my eyes.

I don't know why, but I really needed to hear it.

Though, after what happened last night, I'm not so sure it's true.

"Are you sure you want to do this?" Everly pauses with the tattoo gun just above my skin.

I glance down at the stencil of the script scrawled on my rib cage. The word has a lump forming in my throat. She didn't ask the meaning, and I don't intend to tell her. It's for me and me only. And even though the thought of that needle hitting my virgin skin makes my heart race, it's something I need to do. I suck in a deep breath and nod.

"I'm sure."

She warned me the rib cage was painful, but I can handle

pain. I've already experienced more than I ever thought possible. This will be nothing.

"Okay." Everly presses the needle against my skin, but the pain isn't nearly as sharp or as bad as I anticipated.

Maybe what I've already been through was enough to make me immune to something so small.

"So..." Everly lifts the needle and glances up at me. "Now that you're feeling better and Preacher is almost done finalizing all the plans, you're going to be leaving soon. Are you excited?"

Ay shet.

Acid churns in my stomach. "I've haven't thought about it much, to be honest."

Because I've been so wrapped up in trying to figure out Elijah and too afraid of facing what my new life will be.

She returns to work and nods. "I don't know how much anyone else has told you, but the guys did the same thing for a friend of mine, Liz."

I nod. "Yeah, Preacher mentioned they've done it before. And that she is going to help me, too."

Everly grins. "You'll like Liz, and she'll help you get adjusted to living here and being somewhere new." Her smile falters. "Plus, she's been through something pretty awful. It's not the same thing that happened to you, but she *gets it.*"

After picking up bits and pieces from what Everly and Preacher have told me, I have a pretty good idea of what Everly and Liz suffered. The fact that I'll be with someone who's gone through such a traumatic event and come through on the other side gives me some hope.

But the thought of leaving E, especially after what happened last night, has me swallowing back the bile rising in my throat.

Everly pauses with the needle raised. "You don't look very excited about the prospect of setting up your new life. Are you sure you don't want to reconsider going home?"

I shake my head. "I can't."

One of her dark eyebrows rises. "You really don't think they'll understand?"

I bite my lip. The way she says it makes it sound like everyone back home is heartless and uncaring. It couldn't be further from the truth. "My feelings about it haven't changed. Too much has happened. Too much is broken. My life there is over."

She sighs, and her shoulders slump slightly before she leans down and gets back to work. "I would try to convince you otherwise, but you don't look very happy right now. That have anything to do with E?"

Is there any point lying to her?

She may be able to offer some insight into the man who is so closed off, so unreachable. Last night should have been a turning point. I should have woken this morning in his arms, to a man willing to let me in and allow me to help him move past what happened and his guilt. Instead, all I got was abandoned.

I lean back against the leather headrest of the chair and close my eyes. "He told me what happened to his wife and baby last night."

The needle stops. "Wow. I'm kind of surprised he told you the truth. He doesn't talk to anyone about it."

I'm not about to tell Everly things Elijah told me in confidence and when he was in the middle of some sort of flashback panic attack, but something happened last night, and I need to understand what that is.

My lack of experience with men and relationships makes unraveling what's going on with E even more difficult.

I glance over at her. "He also kissed me."

She freezes, pulls back, and sets the machine down on the small table next to her. "Last night?"

I shake my head. "A few days ago. And then...*I* kissed *him* last night."

A tiny smile tugs at the corner of her lips. "Is that all that happened?"

Not even the tip of the iceberg.

Something life-altering occurred. Something I can't explain or even comprehend myself. I've never felt so safe, so content, so *loved*...And it was in the arms of a man who can never love me because his heart belongs to his dead wife.

I rub at my eyes. "We slept together."

Her jaw drops. "You *what*?"

"No!" I shake my head. "Not like *that*. We didn't have sex. We just literally *slept* together. In the same bed."

"Ooh." She nods slowly and crosses her arms over her chest. "And let me guess, he disappeared this morning without a word, and now you're wondering what the hell happened and what it means?"

I shrug and chuckle softly. "Pretty much."

She sighs and leans back slightly. "I'm gonna tell you something you probably don't want to hear right now. But nothing is easy to understand with these guys. They're all basically emotional children."

A laugh bubbles from my lips. "Preacher doesn't seem like that."

Her lips curl into a smile. "Preacher is probably the most mature in a lot of ways, but he definitely has his faults."

"So, how do you ever understand what's going on in their heads?"

She leans forward and rests her elbows on her knees. "You kind of don't." Her shoulders rise and fall slightly. "I ask him, of course, and I try to get him to talk to me, but sometimes, it's like pulling teeth."

"I can see that."

"And after what E went through with Claire and then his prison time," she shakes her head, "that man has all kinds of demons I can't even imagine warring inside him."

Demons warring inside him.

It's the perfect analogy. Seeing him last night so distraught about what he had done—not only that led to the massive tragedy in his life but also what he did to the men on that ship that brought it all back—proves the true inner turmoil he suffers on a daily basis.

I twist my hands in my lap and stare at them. "Do you ever think he'll be able to move on from it?"

A long silence settles between us, and then finally, Everly reaches out and places her hand over mine. "Oh, honey, that's kind of an impossible question to answer. Every one of us has scars. Some are visible, and some are hidden. Every one of us has demons. Some people defeat their demons or at least manage to keep them locked away somewhere that they don't interfere with daily life. Others feed them, giving them strength and power, and it just leads to them constantly fighting a war they're destined to lose."

"That doesn't make me feel much better."

She squeezes my forearm. "You already got this far yourself in such a short time."

Sometimes it feels like that isn't true at all. "But, I'd be nowhere without all of your help."

She pats my arm, then pushes back and grabs her machine again. "That's okay. Everybody needs help sometimes. And you might be just what Elijah needs."

I might be what he needs?

Here I've been thinking about how much I owe him after what he did for me, what he continues to do for me.

"I think it's the other way around, Everly. I'm the one who needs him right now."

Despite what may have happened last night.

She grins at me and shrugs. "Maybe you need each other."

19

ELIJAH

The sun finally drops beneath the tree line, and I stare out at the pitch-dark blackness of the lake at night. The lighthouse down the beach sends a ray out into the water, a warning for ships to stay the hell back, but otherwise, the stillness is only broken by the sound of the waves lapping against the frozen shore.

I can't stay away much longer.

I've already been gone most of the day in an effort to avoid Eva. Other than sneaking in after she left with Everly to grab a quick shower after my run, I've been M.I.A.—something totally unusual for me. I'm just not ready to confront what happened last night between us or the feelings raging in my body.

I may never be ready.

It's been a decade since I've had someone else in my bed, and yet, it felt so natural to have her in my arms...and to be in hers. The steady rise and fall of her chest pressing into mine and the soft little moans she made in her sleep still echo in my head.

No matter how wrong I knew it was, my body responded to her.

But *it is* wrong. So. Fucking. Wrong.

After everything she's been through, she doesn't need a man pressing his hard cock against her back as she sleeps. She doesn't need a man dreaming about stripping off the T-shirt she's wearing to see her beautiful body and taste every inch of it. She doesn't need that. She doesn't need *me*.

All I can bring her is more pain, and she's had enough of that to last ten lifetimes already. We both have.

And then some.

What she needs is to get away, to start over, to find a way to move on from what happened to her.

And I need to let her without being selfish. Without letting her bear the weight of my guilt. What I did to her last night wasn't fair. She never should have been put in that position, never have seen me in that state. It forced her to step into a situation that doesn't have anything to do with her. It's my burden, and mine alone.

And it's time I started acting like I have my shit together.

I turn and trudge through the snow cover toward the warehouse behind me, ducking my head down against the bitter wind coming off the lake. Another storm is headed this way. One that threatens to dump a massive pile of snow on us.

Normally, that would be annoying, but maybe it's a good thing. A way to cleanse everything and to start over. Whitewash the world and leave a blank slate.

The door stands in front of me, but my hand doesn't want to reach out to enter the code and pull it open. Instead, it shakes at my side. I grab it with my other hand and squeeze tightly.

Get it together. Now, E.

Falling the fuck apart doesn't help *anyone*, least of all Evangeline.

I punch in the code and tug open the door to the warehouse.

The usual congregation point—the massive table in the

center of the space—sits empty, but voices carry from the kitchen, getting louder as I make my way across the concrete floor.

Fuck.

I glance at my watch. They're going to be hungry and crabby. I should've been back to make dinner hours ago. Hopefully, someone picked up my slack since that seems to be the only thing I'm good at and I don't fuck up.

Until now.

The smell of something rich and spicy hits me, and I pause just outside the kitchen.

Damn, that smells good.

I swing the last step into the room, where I spend most of my time. "Who cooked?"

Rion shifts his massive body out of the way, and my growling stomach is replaced by my heart pounding so hard, my chest aches.

Fuck.

Evangeline turns from her spot at the stove and offers me a hesitant smile. "I did. My grandmother's pork adobo recipe. There's still some left. Do you want some?"

I can't seem to find the words *yes* or *no* as I stare at the beautiful woman who held me last night when I had a total of breakdown. The one who brought me back from the deep, dark, bottomless abyss I always fall into after I have to do the things I did last night, anytime I think about what happened to Claire and our baby.

If it weren't for her and the way she walked me through my agony, I don't know how long I would've stayed in that dark place. Too long to be healthy.

But now, I find myself in another one. One of my own making because I let myself develop feelings for this woman.

Footsteps down the hallway have me peering over my shoulder.

Preacher approaches. "I have good news. Where is Evangeline?"

I nod into the kitchen and step to the side so he can enter.

He slips in past me and grins at Eva. "Evangeline, I have almost everything I've been waiting on."

A despair I haven't felt since I lost Claire coils around my lungs, making it impossible to breathe.

That's it. It's over. It's time for Eva to go home.

I squeeze my eyes closed to try to regain some semblance of control. We need to take Erjon out of commission before I'll really feel like she's safe, and the call I made earlier to set up the meeting with him tomorrow hopefully means we'll get what we need to take him out right away.

Once that's done and Preacher has whatever he's still waiting on, she can truly be free.

Her soft, lyrical voice floats across the room. "When do I leave?"

The question is like a knife stabbing into the already shattered pieces of my heart.

I force my eyes open and find Preacher watching me intently. Rion leans against the counter next to Eva and raises an eyebrow as he crosses his arms over his chest.

Preacher clears his throat. "I'll have everything wrapped up in a few days. After that...whenever you're ready to, I guess?"

Instead of looking at him, Eva's gaze meets mine. Her soft eyes are filled with questions, but I don't have any answers. At least, not the ones she's looking for. Not the ones that will give her a happily ever after. And after everything she's been through, she deserves it.

All I have are the broken pieces of what I used to be, of *who* I used to be.

Losing Claire and spending almost a decade in prison has left me without a fucking clue who I am anymore. I can't be someone for her when I'm no one.

I turn and stalk out of the kitchen without a word.

Heavy footsteps follow me down the hallway. "E."

"Rion, don't start with me." I twist back to him and stop.

He holds up his hands in resignation. "I haven't said anything, bro."

"You were about to." I scowl and shove a finger in his massive chest.

"How do you know that?"

"Because I know you," I snarl at him before I turn and make my way down the hall.

He follows me despite my clear warning to back off. "You need to talk to her."

"Who?"

"You know damn well who."

I reach the closed door to my room and turn back to him. "I don't know what you're talking about."

"Oh, cut the bullshit, E." A vein in Rion's temple bulges. "Are you really gonna stand there and try to tell me that you don't feel something for that girl in there? Are you really going to act like she doesn't *mean* something to you?"

"It hasn't even been two weeks."

He snorts and shakes his head. "I think we've established that how much time you spend with somebody really has no fucking bearing whatsoever on how strong your feelings are for them."

He's right about that.

I never thought I'd feel anything for anyone again, and now my entire soul is being torn in two by the thought of that woman leaving. "There's nothing to say, Rion. She has to go."

He raises an eyebrow at me. "She does?"

I scowl at him and twist the doorknob. The door opens, and I step in and turn to slam it in his face.

He shoves his huge knee between the door and the jamb to keep it from closing. "We're not done, E."

"Yes, we are. I have nothing else to say to you."

His lips twist into a sneer. "Then say it to *her*."

"Why the fuck do you care so much? You...who has never had a serious relationship, who has probably slept with more girls than I've even met in my entire lifetime. You...who can't seem to keep his dick in his pants."

He shoves the door the rest of the way open and barges in, his gigantic frame towering over mine. Rion doesn't throw around his weight and size unless he has to, so to do it to one of us means he really is pissed. "Insulting me isn't gonna make you feel any better, E. I know who I am, and I'm comfortable with that, whereas you don't have a fucking clue what's going on and are in denial."

"I'm not in denial about anything."

He snorts and shakes his head. "You say in denial..." He sighs and rubs his eyes before returning his too-knowing gaze to me. "I know this entire situation has to be one giant mind-fuck for you. Dealing with the Albanians again. Having to go in there. Having Eva in your room and up in your head. But just because it's coated in all this high emotion doesn't mean that what you're feeling for her isn't real." He waves out toward the warehouse. "Look at War and Grace. I didn't want her here. I didn't believe that what they had was going to last. None of us did. We all thought it was an emotionally charged reaction to the emotionally charged situation. But look at them now."

I slam my palm into the wall next to me. "Look at *me* now." I run my stinging hand over myself. "I'm a fucking mess. I'm not in any position to offer that girl anything."

"That's where you're wrong, E. That girl literally has nothing. Not even her name anymore. You can offer her everything. You just have to do it. You have to be willing to open yourself up to the potential."

"I can't do that."

My response comes so quickly, he clenches his jaw and

wraps his hands around the edge of the doorjamb. "'Cuz you're a stubborn asshole."

"I could say the same to you."

"Yeah," he nods, "but the difference is...I admit it." He shoves off the door and storms off toward his room. His door slams, the sound vibrating through the hallway and back down to me.

Fucking know-it-all prick.

He can never keep his nose out of everyone else's business. It's fucking ridiculous, especially since the man has never cared about a woman his entire damn life for anything more than being a warm, wet hole to stick his cock into.

I grab the door to slam it, but Eva's soft footsteps freeze me in place.

Close the door now and shut her out forever.

It would be so easy to do. Just close the door and turn the lock.

They would find somewhere else for her to sleep. They would make sure she gets out of here and set up with her new life okay without any help from me.

It would be so fucking easy, yet, I make no movement to do it.

Fear and longing keep me frozen with my hand on the door. She appears in the hallway in front of me. Her long, dark, impossibly shiny hair flows over her shoulders and down her back, and the cream-colored sweater she borrowed from one of the girls only emphasizes the beautiful bronze tone of her skin and the vibrant hazel of her eyes.

Fuck, she's beautiful.

It's probably why they took her.

She deserves someone better than me, someone whole, but she also deserves an explanation before I kick her the fuck out.

"Come in."

Her eyes widen slightly, like she wasn't expecting me to ask, and she pulls her lip between her teeth as she cautiously steps forward to the door and past me.

I let the door close behind her and turn to face the woman who has thrown my world into utter chaos since I first laid eyes on her on that ship.

She faces me and twists her hands nervously in front of her. "So...I'm going to go soon."

Christ, it's even worse when the words come from those lips.

My chest tightens, and I rub it and nod while trying my best not to look at her. I can't stand here and pretend I don't care that she's leaving.

"Preacher said he needs a few days. Then...whenever I'm ready." She pauses for a moment, undoubtedly waiting for some reaction from me. "And...I don't think there's any reason not to go as soon as he has everything ready."

I keep my eyes averted. Originally, I hadn't planned on telling her where we are going tomorrow, what we are doing, but she needs it for peace of mind as much as I do. "We're going to see Erjon tomorrow, to scope out the place and his men, so we know how we can best handle the mission. It won't take long for us to form a plan and act. Once he and his crew are gone, any vestiges of the group that took you will be destroyed. Anyone who knew you were taken will be dead. Then, you'll be truly safe."

"And then...I'll leave."

I grit my teeth and nod, forcing myself to finally meet her eyes. "And then...you leave."

She stares at me, unshed tears shimmering in her gaze. "That's what you want? You want me to leave?"

"Fuck, Eva." I throw my hands up and move to the far side of the room away from her. "No, that's not what I fucking want," I scrub my hands over my face, "and that's the entire problem. I *can't* want you."

"Why not?"

Her question is nothing more than a whisper, but it slams into me like a tidal wave.

I turn back to her, to ensure she sees the conviction in what I'm about to say. "Because you deserve so much more than a broken man, an ex-con, a *killer*. You deserve everything you've always dreamed about, and it sure as hell isn't a guy like me."

"No." Her bottom lip quivers as she approaches me. She stops a few steps away and shakes her head. The wide neck of the sweater she wears slips to one side, exposing her collarbone and one slim shoulder. "It wasn't a guy like you. It was a guy like the one who sold me to the Albanians."

20

EVANGELINE

Finally saying the words out loud to him feels like releasing the pressure and the weight I've been carrying on my shoulders and chest since he first rescued me.

The girls told me I should tell him the truth about why I can't go back, and maybe he needs to know to understand why I want to stay now.

His blue eyes darken and narrow on me. "What are you talking about?"

He thinks some sort of monster stole me off the street. That one of those creepy and sinister Albanians is responsible. The truth is so much worse. So much more devastating than he can imagine.

I wander over to the window and pull back the blinds to stare out at the forest around the warehouse and the small glimpses of the lake beyond it that peek through. The moon reflects off the water, breaking the pitch-black dark of night. Crystals of snow and ice cover the trees and the ground. The white world sends goose bumps across my skin.

"The girls told me I should tell you the truth. About why I can't go back. So, I'm going to."

No matter how painful it is.

No matter how much I never want to say the words out loud again.

"I was always a good girl. My parents are very strict Catholics, which is pretty common in the area that we live in. I always followed their rules and the rules of the Church, the rules of God. And in many ways, they're still very old school." It's so hard for people who didn't grow up in that environment to understand. "They busted their butts working to send me to private Catholic school so that I can make something of myself and get an education. But at the same time, they still believed in a lot of older cultural traditions. Like arranged marriages."

I don't look back at him. I don't want to see his reaction to that.

Most people see it as a sexist, antiquated idea that a person isn't able to choose who they're going to spend the rest of their life with. But where I'm from, it's not. It's a tradition. One respected and upheld and believed in.

"My parents met and married that way, and they eventually fell in love with each other. That's always the hope. That it will be a good match. An arrangement that leads to a real connection, either before the wedding or after." My stomach churns. This is the part of the story that will be the hardest, the point at which I broke down when I told Valentina and Everly. "We had a family friend...people who had been friends of my parents for decades. Their son, Danilo, was three years older than me and still unmarried. He was handsome and charming and funny, and any number of girls would have bent over backward to have been matched with him, but for some reason, his parents chose me."

How different would things have been if they hadn't?

I wouldn't have been taken. I wouldn't have spent weeks in Hell on that ship. And I wouldn't have met Elijah...

"I was in my last semester at the University of Southeastern

Philippines, about to get my degree in library sciences, and I wanted to wait until I graduated for the wedding. He said he understood, and he was supportive of my desire to finish my education. He was always very thoughtful and attentive when we were together, but as custom called for, we were rarely, if ever, alone. There were a lot of chaperoned dates. But the night I was taken..." Emotion clogs my throat, and I struggle to swallow past it. "He was supposed to meet me outside the library to walk me home. Only, he didn't. He led me straight into the hands of one of those men you killed on the ship instead."

Even without turning around, Elijah's anger burns into me. I can feel his stare over every centimeter of my skin.

"The man handed him a large envelope I can only assume was filled with money. I begged Danilo to help me, and...it's like he was a totally different person from the one I'd known my entire life." A switch flipped, and the man I thought was falling in love with me became a monster. I squeeze my eyes closed against the image of that sinister grin spreading over his face. "He just laughed."

Tears flow down my cheeks, and I struggled to find the words to continue with my story. For some reason, it's so much harder to tell E than it was to tell the girls. Maybe because I know what he'll think—that I was a stupid, naïve child to believe Danilo cared for me, and I walked right into what happened to me.

"The man who took me asked Danilo if he was sure I was a virgin."

E's sharp intake of breath and low growl fill the room.

"Danilo told the man he was positive, and I heard the man say that's the only reason they were giving him as much. Because of what I would bring on the market as a virgin."

Bile climbs up my throat, and I swallow it and wipe away more tears. "My fiancé laughed and said he knew that and couldn't believe his luck when his parents betrothed him to me. The way he was talking," I squeeze my eyes shut and breathe slowly, "he acted like he had done this before. I don't know how many other girls fell victim to him, but there are other girls missing from the area we lived in."

Women who probably suffered the same fate I was facing if not for these men.

Or worse.

And he's still back there, probably doing it to another innocent woman.

E doesn't say anything. Not that I expect him to.

The story ripped open every wound I have and left me standing here in front of the window bleeding. He knows it all now, and his opinion of me has to have changed.

How could it not after hearing how stupid I was?

A minute passes.

Then another.

I gather up enough courage to turn and face him.

He stands nearly a foot away from me, his fists clenched at his sides, and his jaw gritted hard enough to make a vein in his neck throb. "Jesus, Evangeline, why didn't you tell me?"

"I didn't know how to." I shrug. "And I was embarrassed that I was so stupid."

He closes the distance between us, pulls me into his arms, and buries his face in my hair. "You weren't stupid, Eva. You just trusted somebody who was supposed to protect you, who was supposed to love you. That's not stupid. That's human nature." He pulls back and tips my face up. "And when they fail you, or even worse, betray you, that makes it hurt even more."

"That's why you can't stop feeling guilty for what happened to Claire, even though it wasn't your fault."

He stares down at me with darkly ominous eyes and slides one thumb across my lips. "You'll never convince me that what happened wasn't my fault, Eva. I've had too many years of blaming myself to stop now. But don't compare your situation to mine because it's absolutely not the same."

"I don't see it any differently. And now, you understand why I can't go back. My parents...the guilt they would feel over what happened and the position they put me in with him would be too much."

Concern flickers in his gaze. "And what about what they're feeling right now, not knowing what happened to you? Do you want them to live with that the rest of their lives?"

The tears fall in earnest now, and I shake my head. "No, I don't, but I also don't how to tell them I'm not coming back and that Danilo was responsible for what happened."

"You'll think of something. You need to call them."

I take a deep breath. "I will. Just not right now."

Not until I know what I'll say without destroying them.

He shakes his head. "And what about the man who sold you? Your fiancé? Do you want him to be able to hurt another woman like this?"

"I thought you were dismantling the organization?"

He nods. "We are, but it's not the only one by any stretch of the imagination. Other men will step up right in its place."

I fight the urge to vomit at the thought of another woman suffering what I did. But I also know I can't face him again, can't make public what happened to me. "I can't go back there to testify against him."

A tiny smile pulls at the corners of E's mouth. One that lacks humor and holds a sinister edge. "That wasn't exactly what I had in mind."

"What do you mean?"

He sighs and pulls me into his chest. "Let's just say Cutter has some connections who can take care of it and make it so he can never hurt anyone again."

Yet again, I find myself in the position where I should feel some guilt or concern that E has basically just told me they're going to kill Danilo, but all that fills my heart is contentment at being in E's arms and fear of never being here again.

The warmth of his chest pressed against mine. The smell of his skin. The way he holds me so tightly.

How do I walk away from that?

I pull back and tip my face up to look at him. "Do you understand now?"

Moonlight streams in from the window, lighting one side of his face while leaving the other in shadow. It's such a perfectly fitting state for him—half light and half dark. A contradiction through and through.

"You may not be what I always dreamed of E, but you're my anchor point. You are what's keeping me from losing myself and completely falling apart through all that's happened. You've held me steady and kept me from drifting away in the storm of despair surrounding me. You made me believe I can have a new life."

He brushes his thumb across my cheeks. "I shouldn't be, Eva. An anchor may be able to save you in a storm, but it can also drag you down. It can hold you underwater while you're running out of air. It can drown you. You don't want me to be your anchor. You deserve more, and I don't deserve you."

Irritation has me pulling out of his touch. "I'm the one who should decide what I deserve, E, and you need to stop beating yourself up over something that happened a decade ago that you had no control over. She made a choice to be with you, knowing what you were doing. She took that risk, too. Stop making yourself miserable just so you feel something other than missing her."

I wait for him to fly off into a rage. For his face to redden at my audacity and his hands to curl into fists, ready to lash out at something over my words.

Instead, his shoulders sag, and he shakes his head gently.

"Christ, Eva..." He steps forward, and his lips descend on mine in a demanding crush, stealing my breath.

My arms tighten around him, and he moves one hand down to my hip to drag me up against him fully. Heat surges through my body and centers between my legs. A dull, throbbing ache builds, one that has my hips pushing against him. His hand drops from my hip and slips inside my yoga pants, his calloused fingers running over my smooth skin, leaving goose bumps in their wake. He works it around the front of my body and down between my legs to cup the sensitive area there.

I moan into his mouth and dig my fingers through his hair as I struggle to get even closer to him. His tongue thrashes against mine, and he walks me backward until my knees hit the bed.

He lowers me gently, kissing his way down my neck and across the *V* of my exposed collarbone in the sweater. I scrape my hands against the back of his neck and shift toward him. His cock rubs between my legs, and a jolt of pleasure ripples through my body.

Oh, God...

I moan and curl up around him, and his mouth returns to mine for a slow, languid kiss.

He pulls back and searches my face. "Are you sure this is what you want, Eva? I can't offer you more."

What does that mean?

In this moment, it doesn't even matter. After everything I've been through, I just want Elijah to *be* with me. I need him to hold me, to love me in a way no man ever has before. I need to feel alive again, and not just like I'm weeding through day after day, waiting for something else bad to happen.

This is something good. Something incredible. And something I so desperately need.

"Yes." I manage to gasp out the word. "I'm sure."

I want to lose myself in the belief that we can be together, even if it's a lie. I just want *him*.

My answer seems to satisfy him. His eyes darken with something that sets off a blaze inside me—lust. He works my pants down and off and then shifts up to grab the hem of my shirt. He pulls it up and over my head and stills as he stares down at me in nothing but a bra and panties.

"Christ, you're beautiful, Eva."

The compliment sends a rush of warmth and pride through my body.

This man thinks I'm beautiful.

With all the places he's been, all the things he's seen and done, a woman like me is still beautiful to him.

His gaze narrows on my ribcage, and he brushes a finger gently over the fresh tattoo. "*Malaya?* What does that mean?"

I hadn't anticipated anyone asking. It's for me, a reminder that where I've been and what I've been through is in the past, and I'm in control of my own future.

"Freedom."

His eyes meet mine, the blue darkening to midnight. He runs his fingers over it one more time, and a tiny smile tugs at his lips. "Perfect."

He grabs for the hem of his shirt and pulls it up and off in one quick motion, exposing the smooth expanse of his inked skin. *Valhalla* dominates his chest in thick scrollwork, and a myriad of colorful words and images cover his arms. Someday, I'll explore them all and ask him for the stories behind each one, but not tonight.

Tonight isn't about his past and where he's been. It's about now.

He reaches for the buttons of his jeans, flips it open, and lowers the zipper. My eyes travel with his hand. I did my best not to look the other night, not to invade his privacy by looking at him when he was so distraught.

It was the last thing on my mind then.

But now...it's the only thing.

I can't drag my eyes away from the beauty of his taut muscles bulging and rippling as he works his jeans down and off his body, letting his hard cock spring free. I gulp against my dry throat and stare at it shamelessly.

He's so beautiful.

He plants his knee on the bed and lowers his head into my line of vision. "Eva? Are you all right?"

I nod slowly and reach out tentatively to brush my fingers over the scar on his ribcage, where he took the shot when he went to take out the Albanians. He doesn't stop me as my hand drifts lower, down over the chiseled *V* of muscle that leads straight to his erection.

He freezes, and I circle my hand around it and squeeze gently. His eyes slam shut, and he grits his teeth together.

I release him immediately. "I'm sorry."

His eyes fly open again. "For what?"

"Whatever I just did wrong."

"Jesus, Eva." He drops down onto one elbow over me and captures my face in his other palm to plant a deep, slow, lingering kiss to my lips. "You didn't do anything wrong. I just haven't been touched by a woman in a long fucking time, and it feels so damn good."

"Oh."

I had imagined him drowning his sorrows in a line of women he could have mindless sex with when he was released from prison, but apparently, that couldn't be further from the truth.

He lowers his hand from my face down behind my back to unhook my bra and pulls it off, exposing my breasts to the cool air of the room. He cups one and brushes his thumb across the hard nipple.

"Oh, my God." I groan and rock my pelvis against his as pleasure shoots straight between my legs.

What was that?

It's like a direct line between the two, and when he leans down and sucks it between his lips, my hips fly off the bed. The only thing holding me in place is his hard body pressing down against mine.

His hands drift down to the waistband of my panties, and he tugs on them and works them over my thighs, letting his fingers linger on my sensitive skin. I shudder at the light touch, and he shifts back and pulls them off my legs.

I've never felt so exposed and so beautiful as I do right now, watching Elijah's gaze linger over my body.

He repositions himself over me and kisses me while his fingers glide through the wetness between my legs. A deep, coiling tension I've never felt before builds low in my belly, and my hips move up to grind against his hand. He kisses along my collarbone and up my neck and captures my mouth again as he slips a finger inside me.

A gasp tumbles from my lips, and I drop my head back while my body arches up to him.

He growls low in my ear. "Christ, Eva. You're so wet."

I nod slowly, and his fingers move magically inside me, drawing me closer to something cataclysmic.

My hips roll against his hand—harder and faster—and a scalding heat explodes through my body. I gasp and jerk against him, clenching around his finger. White-hot light flashes against my lids, and pleasure ripples through my limbs. He captures my moans in his mouth and slowly lowers me back down to the bed as I finally come down from Heaven.

"What the hell was that?" I gasp as my body spasms.

His brow rises, and then he narrows his eyes. "Have you never had an orgasm before?"

A flush of embarrassment climbs over my chest, neck, and

cheeks, and I try to bury my face in my hands, but he pulls it away.

"Eva, are you..." he pauses and considers his words for a moment, "are you *still* a virgin?"

It's the obvious question after what I told him and what he saw when he rescued me. I haven't wanted to go into detail about what happened on that ship...for many reasons.

I bite my lip, and he pulls his hand away from me and settles over me.

"Yeah, I was too valuable for them to do...*that*."

He squeezes his eyes closed and clenches his jaw. "Jesus."

"They made me do...*other things* on that ship. Things I never want to talk about or remember. But not *that*."

He keeps his eyes closed for a moment then opens them slowly to stare down at me. Something dark overtakes his gaze, and he shakes his head. "I can't do this, Eva. I just can't."

21

ELIJAH

I push up to pull away from her, to put space between her and myself. Space I need to clear my head and get my shit together, so I'm not tempted to do something stupid. Like actually go through with what we've started.

But her small, warm hand curls around my bicep, keeping me in place, hovering over her with my hard cock pressed between us.

Every muscle in my body tightens. My blood rushes in my ears.

Those hazel eyes that have always shown me everything in her beautiful soul stare back at me with such confusion and pain, it makes my chest physically hurt. "Please, Elijah. I want this."

God, she's so innocent. So completely oblivious to why this can't happen.

She doesn't grasp that this is just her body overpowering her brain. Her sexual need trying to push away the voice that should be telling her to stop. She doesn't have the benefit of experience in controlling her body's reactions.

And now, she thinks this is about me not wanting her.

It couldn't be further from the truth.

I sit back, as much as her grip will allow, and rub my hand on the back of my neck. "That's not the problem, sweetheart. You should be saving yourself for somebody who deserves you. Somebody who's going to stick around and treat you right. I can't be that. Not now and not ever."

Even if I wanted to be, which I don't. I can't want that. It's something I gave up on a long time ago. Something I haven't earned the right to have again.

Space.

I need space. I need to not have my aching cock pressing against her soft skin. I need the temptation of this very willing *virgin* far, far away from me.

Her hand tightens around my arm, and she sits up until our faces are mere inches from each other. "I may not know what I'm doing in this bed, Elijah, but I know what I'm doing *here*. I know who you are." She presses her hand over my heart. "Here."

The warm flutter of her breath across my lips practically calls out to me to kiss her. To show her she has no idea what she's asking for.

She leans forward and presses a kiss against my chest—a soft caress of lips that sends my heart stuttering. "You're the man who rescued me. You could've left me on that ship and walked away. You could've let me die. Because I probably would have before the Coast Guard ever got there. You could have listened to your friends when they told you to leave me there. But you didn't. Because this," she presses her hand against me tighter and curls her fingers into my skin, her nails biting into the flesh, "wouldn't let you walk away. Don't walk away now just because of some misplaced belief about your worth or my honor. After what happened to me, after what I've been through, this is all I want. *You* are all I want."

Fuck.

Every word spreads the crack in my wall of resolve open a little. I've spent so long building it up and hiding behind it, keeping myself from ever caring about or getting close to anyone else again, for fear of what they would do to me, and even more so, what I might do to them. It's been my constant companion, shielding me from acknowledging I care. But Eva chipped into it the first time our eyes locked and has slowly worked at breaking it down with every moment we've spent together.

How am I supposed to deny her what we both want? How do I turn and walk away from the longing and need in her gaze? How do I leave the one thing that has made me feel anything other than pain in so damn long?

She leans forward and presses her lips to mine, and her small hand circles my cock again tentatively before I can muster up the willpower to leave. I groan against her mouth, and my fingers dig into her hips.

Christ.

So soft.

So gentle.

So trusting.

So damn wrong for me.

I've done everything I can for the last decade to punish myself for what I did, to make myself feel as awful every day as I did that day with Claire's blood on my hands, but with Eva's soft, warm body pressed against mine, I have to be selfish just once.

When this is over and she's gone, I can go back to my misery, back to the self-flagellation, back to my hole. But for a few hours tonight, I can live again. I can remember what it's like to be touched by someone who cares, by someone who needs me as much as I need them.

My cock twitches between us, and she shifts forward to straddle my lap. Her pussy, still wet from her orgasm, glides along my length, and she moans into my mouth. Her tongue snakes out tentatively to run along the seam of my lips. I let her explore, let her lead and find the way. Let her unleash all the passion she has inside her because if I let loose, she won't be able to handle what I have to give her.

Her nails score across my shoulder blades, and I reach between us and grasp my cock. It throbs in my hand, and I drag the head through her hot, wet pussy. She gasps and rocks her hips against mine, positioning me at her opening, practically begging me to enter her.

Shit.

I grit my teeth, pull back, and lock eyes with her. This is her chance to see it. To look into my eyes and figure out this isn't what she wants. For her to remember who I am. But instead of stopping, she slowly lowers herself down on me in an agonizing slide that tests every ounce of self-control I contain.

Every muscle in my body tenses.

Don't thrust up. Don't thrust up. Don't thrust up.

Each tiny shift of her hips, every centimeter lower she goes, I grit my teeth harder. So hard, my teeth might crack. I dig my hands into her soft flesh, guiding her down slowly, so she doesn't hurt herself and torturing myself at the same time.

A tiny mewl slips from her lips. She closes her eyes and drops back her head, thrusting her breasts forward toward my all-too-eager mouth.

"Are you okay?"

She nods and shoves her hips down to fully impale herself on my cock.

"Sweet fuck..." I drop my forehead against her chest, then pull her body against mine and suck her taut nipple between my lips. The soft, clean taste of her skin makes my mouth water.

She groans and shifts up a few inches before lowering herself back down gradually.

Fuck if this isn't the best feeling in the world.

Her hot, wet pussy wrapped around my dick. Her hard nipple rolling over my tongue. Her soft skin brushing against mine.

I let her nipple free from my lips with a pop and kiss my way up her neck and to her ear to nip at the lobe. She groans, clenches around me, and rolls her hips in a circular motion that has my balls drawing up and threatening to explode.

My hand reaches back to her long, dark hair, and I tug her head back gently, forcing her face up to mine. Her lust-soaked gaze meets mine.

I thrust up to meet her downward glide. "Keep doing that, and this isn't gonna last very long."

Even in the dim room only lit by a thin line of moonlight peeking in through the window, the satisfied grin on her lips at my words stops my breath.

She's fucking happy.

After all she's been through, she's fucking happy with me buried inside of her and with the realization that she has me on the edge of control.

Eva may have been a virgin, but she knows exactly what she's doing to me now. She pushes up until only the head of my cock remains inside of her then pushes herself down hard and fast, driving me up so far inside her, it feels like coming home.

"Fuck."

I can't take it anymore.

My restraint finally snaps, unleashing everything that's been pent up inside me since I first pulled her into my arms on that ship. Releasing who I really am. *What* I really am.

I roll her onto her back and take her mouth with another searing kiss while driving my cock into her hard and deep. She gasps, and her eyes fly open. I thrust into her again, pushing her toward another release and me closer to utter bliss. Something I haven't experienced in so fucking long, I've forgotten how good it feels.

Her legs wrap around my waist, and she digs her heels into my lower back, driving me forward on every thrust and begging me to come back on every retreat.

She tugs at my hair and rolls her hips up to meet mine. Our bodies move together fluidly, like waves on the water, rolling and cresting, a beautiful symphony of two broken people becoming one for a moment in time.

Her limbs shake, and a tingle at the base of my spine warns me of my impending release. I shift my position slightly so the head of my cock will drag along her G-spot while my pelvis grinds against her clit. She gasps and arches back, then her mouth falls open.

Watching Eva come a second time sends a rush of heat spreading through my body. Her pussy ripples and clenches around my shaft, and it's all I need to completely lose my self-control.

I drive into her over and over, until I finally release everything I've been holding onto in a hard rush inside her. It's like a thousand-pound weight has been pulled from my chest, and I can finally breathe again. For a split-second, the world isn't the dark, harsh place it has been for so long. It's filled with a bright light that was snuffed out so cruelly from my life.

It's peace.

She sags back on the bed, her body twitching slightly, and I lower myself onto her then roll to the side, bringing her with me.

I stare at her eyes, still closed, and breathe in the soft pants coming from between her parted lips. Each one brings the reality of the situation closer and closer to the surface.

Fuck, I hope I didn't hurt her.

I brush her dark, sweat-dampened hair from her forehead and lean forward to press a kiss there. "Are you okay?"

Her lips curl into a grin, and she nods slowly and tightens herself around my cock still embedded deep inside her. I groan and bury my face against her neck. Her pussy clenches tightly again, and ripples of pleasure course through my body.

I kiss her softly, and the taste of her skin on my lips has my heart flip-flopping wildly.

In only a matter of days, I'm going to have to say goodbye to her, goodbye to this.

Her heartbeat slows against mine, and her breathing evens out into the soft rhythm of sleep. I brush my fingers over her pink cheeks and then squeeze my eyes closed.

I thought what I let happen to Claire was the ultimate betrayal. She trusted me, and I got her killed, but what Eva and I just did might have moved to the top of that list.

Because even though my heart is begging me to tell her to stay, I'm going to make her go.

But first, I'm going to kill every motherfucker responsible for what happened to her and anyone who ever had a role in the trafficking business—no matter how small. I'll take them all out with my bare hands if I have to.

Even if I die trying.

22

EVANGELINE

"Are you sure you don't mind if I take these?"

Everly waves a dismissive hand from where she leans against the door jamb, watching me pack the clothes the girls have given me into the suitcase she brought. "Of course not. Keep everything. And when you get to Liz, she'll take you shopping for a real wardrobe and anything else you need."

I sigh, fold another shirt, and tuck it into the corner of the suitcase. Milo lifts his head from his perch near my pillow, but then he drops it again and closes his eyes.

The unease that's plagued me since I first awoke returns full force. "I'm still really uncomfortable with all this."

"With all what?"

I point to the suitcase. "Everything you guys have given me. The money..."

It's still hard to believe they're offering to basically set me up for life. We always struggled for money, and after watching Ma and Pa work so hard to provide for us, it's hard to imagine people I barely know just handing over that kind of money to me for no reason.

She presses her lips together and considers me for a

moment. "Don't be. Everyone here wants to help you any way we can."

"I know." They've been repeating it to me for weeks, trying to make me believe it's true. "But I've done nothing to deserve it."

Everly rolls her eyes. "Stop it. People can help you just because you need help. There doesn't always have to be some ulterior motive."

I wish I could believe that, but what happened with Danilo has left me uneasy about putting my future in anyone else's hands. There's no way to know if or when they'll decide I'm a liability and dump me on my own somewhere I have no connections or ability to support myself. I don't think they will. The girls would never let that happen, but it still bounces around my head.

Footsteps approach in the hallway, and my heart leaps into my throat for a second.

It's not him.

For hours, I've been practically pulling off my skin, waiting for news about E's meeting with Erjon. Rion, Cutter, Warwick, and he have only been gone three hours, but it might as well be twenty.

This could go badly in so many different ways. He could lose control and do or say something stupid. He could get them all killed.

And no matter how many times Grace, Everly, and Preacher have tried to assure me that they know what they're doing and will be okay, I have a hard time believing it now that I know the full truth, the whole story. Now that I've seen Elijah completely fall apart, I'm not so confident he'll be able to keep it together when faced with the man in charge of the entire trafficking operation.

Not after last night.

My body still aches in the best way possible, and my skin

still tingles with a rush of heat and goose bumps, remembering the ghost of his touch floating all over me.

He was rough and hurried. Slow and gentle. Passionate and desperate.

And this morning, when the first light of day snuck in through the curtains, our night of bliss was over...

The bubble around us that kept out everything else that was happening for a few hours burst. Reality slapped me square in the face the moment my eyes opened and I found E tense next to me in bed with a cold look of determination in his eyes.

He was no longer the man who gave himself over to me. He was back to being the man with a dark past. The man who was on a mission to ensure he paid for the rest of his life for what happened. The man who was going to make me leave.

And he walked out that door to meet with the monster Erjon without so much as a goodbye.

Preacher appears next to Everly and leans in to press a kiss to her temple. He waves a large manila envelope in his hand. "The guys are almost there...and I have everything for you, Eva."

He enters and lowers himself onto the bed next to the suitcase. He pets Milo's head for a moment, and his dark eyes flick over to Everly before returning to me. He opens the envelope and pulls out several small items first. "Driver's license, passport, Social Security card." He holds them out to me.

I take them with a shaky hand and stare down at the photo of myself I posed for only a few days ago, now on a license. "Kansas?" I raise an eyebrow.

Preacher smiles and nods. "That's where Liz ended up settling, and that's where you're heading. It's far away from most of the dark shit in our world. Good Midwestern town and good Midwestern people."

Evangeline Divata.

Getting used to a new last name isn't going to be easy, but at least by picking Ma's maiden name, I'm still able to maintain that family connection.

"And I won't have any problem using any of these if I want to apply for a job or open a bank account or anything?"

He reaches into the envelope again and pulls out another stack of documents. "Birth certificate, fake work history and diploma, and no, you won't have any problem doing any of those things. But..." he glances over at Everly and shifts uncomfortably in his seat, "really, Eva, you don't need to work and don't need to worry about setting up a bank account. I've already done that for you. And I already wired $50,000 to get you started."

"What?" I choke on my next breath and cough. "$50,000?"

The room spins a little, and Preacher reaches out to steady me.

I open and close my mouth, trying to find the words. "You have to be joking."

He shakes his head and removes his hand from where it had been holding me at my hip. "We don't want you to have to worry about anything for a long time. That should get you a car and be enough to keep you comfortable for a while. We've already bought the house you're living in, so there's no rent, and Liz knows how to get a hold of us when you need more."

More?

I drop down onto the bed on the opposite side of the suitcase, set the stack of documents he gave me on top of the clothes that aren't mine, and bury my face in my hands. "This is too much." I shake my head. "This is all just too much."

Preacher's large hand finds my shoulder. "Just let us do this for you, Eva. It'll make everyone, especially E, feel better if we know you're safe and taken care of."

I jerk my head up. "Did he say that?"

He tosses another furtive glance at Everly. "Not in so many words but—"

"But nothing." I shove to my feet and rake my hands back through my hair. "I wish everyone would stop pretending like it really matters to him what happens to me. He won't think about me again once I'm gone."

Whereas I will be thinking about him every moment of every day for the rest of my life.

Preacher snorts and shakes his head. Humor brightens his gaze. "That couldn't be further from the truth, doll. I've haven't seen him this twisted up, well...ever. Not even on the anniversary of Claire's death. You matter to him, and he's going to want you safe and cared for."

Why can't he do that? Why can't he keep me safe and take care of me? Why can't I stay here with these people and figure things out with that complicated man? Why do I have to go?

You know why...

I *have* to go. I just don't want to admit it to myself.

Elijah may care about what happens to me. He may feel some sort of responsibility for me because he's the one who rescued me, but there's nothing more than that. He'll never open himself up again the way he did to me last night and the night before that in the shower. Those were flukes brought on by a rush of emotions.

He's making himself very clear about what he wants. Me gone. He may want me enough to fill a need temporarily, to vent at in a way he can't with anyone else, but not enough to keep me here permanently.

Once I accept that fact, things will be a lot easier.

Everly enters the room and steps in front of me. "Have you given any more thought to calling your parents?"

The question tightens my chest. It's been banging around my head relentlessly, the fact that they're worrying and thinking the worst. Maybe it's time to end their suffering as much as it is to end my own where Elijah is concerned.

"I have."

"And?"

"And...I want to call them."

Everly raises a dark eyebrow. "Now?"

I hadn't meant *now*. I'm not sure I'm prepared to hear their voices and to lie to them about where I am and why I'm never coming back. But I can't let them suffer any longer, and it's better to get it over with sooner rather than later.

And maybe it'll take my mind off worrying about Elijah.

Preacher's phone dings in his pocket, and he digs it out. His brow rises, and he pushes to his feet. He looks from Everly to me. "They're there. Going in now."

Shit.

I'm not ready. Not even a little bit. I'm not emotionally prepared to handle what might happen to Elijah in there.

I hold out my hand. "Everly, give me your phone so I can make this call."

If E doesn't come back, I won't be in any shape to make it later.

I don't say that part out loud, but I'm sure Everly understands. Her man is here, safe from harm and mine...

No. He's not mine. That's the whole point.

She digs in her pocket and places her phone in my hand and squeezes gently. "Come find me if you need me. I'll probably be up with Grace."

I nod and hold the phone in my shaky hand. Everly follows Preacher out into the hallway.

It might be hours before we know what happens to Elijah and the guys. I need to keep it together long enough to make this call, then I'll go up and wait with the girls.

Wait for a man who wants nothing to do with me.

My hands shake as I dial the familiar number. Each ring in my ear drives a knife into my heart. I'm going to have to lie to them. I'm going to have to in order to save them from the truth, which is far more hurtful.

I run a hand over Milo's warm, soft fur, and he shifts slightly to expose his stomach for a belly rub. This dang dog is so calm and even keeled. I wish I could say the same.

"Hello?" Pa's familiar voice steals my ability to speak. "Hello?"

Oh, God...

I suck in a breath and clear my throat. "Pa, it's me."

"Eva? Where have you been? Are you all right?" The panic and excitement in his voice almost shatters my will not to return, but if he knew the truth, his joy would fade.

"I'm fine, Pa. Is Ma home?"

"No. She's at church. We've been so worried. Everyone has been searching for you. Where are you?"

I can't give him details, not now, and maybe not ever. "I'm in the United States. I'm sorry I left without telling you."

"Left? Why would you leave and make us worry?"

The lie comes quickly, and far more easily than I ever thought it could, probably because of the truth underlying the words. "I'm so sorry, Pa. I met someone...someone I fell in love with." I bite back a sob and stare at the pillow where Elijah's head lay last night. "I couldn't marry Danilo, and I didn't know how to tell you. So...I left to come here and be with him." I swallow thickly before my final words. "And I'm not coming back."

A silence hangs on the line, one filled with the unspoken disappointment and anger from him.

Finally, he releases a heavy sigh. "You left without a word. Without so much as a goodbye. We thought you had been taken, maybe killed. Now you are telling me we will never see you again? Are you trying to hurt us?"

The sobs I've been holding back finally break out. "I'm so sorry, Pa. I love you and Ma so much. I'm sorry I hurt you like this. I...I didn't think you'd understand. I thought it was for the best this way."

"For the best? Your mother hasn't stopped crying. We've barely slept. Everyone is looking for you. The police."

I shake my head and wipe my eyes. "I know. I wish I would have handled it differently." There's nothing else I can say. No other explanation I can give him. It's probably a good thing Ma isn't home. I'm not sure I could maintain this lie talking to her. "I wanted to let you know I'm all right. I'll call again soon."

If he has anything else to say, I don't hear it. I can't bear to hear how disappointed or angry he is. I end the call and bury my face in my hands.

There's a good chance I'll never go home again. I drop onto the bed and unload everything I've been holding in when it comes to my decision to stay. All the people, the things I'm leaving behind.

The tears flow so hard, the pillow under me is soaked by the time I turn onto my back and stare up at the ceiling.

That is it. I've said my goodbye to that life.

And tomorrow, I'll enter my new one.

23

ELIJAH

The aviators cover Cutter's eyes, but they don't block him from seeing everything, taking in every single detail, assessing the shit out of any situation we get ourselves into.

We're all counting on that as we walk into the familiar club. It's the only reason to enter the viper pit, especially unarmed. There was no point in trying to get a weapon in. Erjon's men will never let us get near that back hallway, let alone into his office, without thoroughly searching all of us.

I'd love to come in and kill him right now, but this is a reconnaissance mission. To get the lay of the land so when we come back, guns blazing, we know exactly who and what we're up against.

These men are the epitome of evil, and having to pretend I want back in is like tearing out a piece of my soul. But sometimes, doing things you don't want to is necessary to survive.

And this is about more than just *me*.

This is about Evangeline's survival. Her future. The new life she deserves. This is about ensuring she won't ever look over her shoulder again or live in constant fear that one day, one of these bastards will hunt her down and remove the possibility she might ever identify any of them. This is about *her*. The woman who has me so twisted into knots, I haven't been able to take a full breath in days.

I hold it now, and every step farther that I take into the club coils the tension in my body tighter. Even having Cutter beside me and Rion and Warwick at my back can't alleviate the feeling of dread sitting like a rock in my stomach.

The same huge, dark-haired goon who sat at the bar last time we were here now stands near the back hallway. His eyes never leave us as we approach. I step up to him and force more conviction than I actually feel in my words. "We're here to see Erjon."

He eyes me, then scans over Rion and Warwick, ending on Cutter. His lips twist into a sneer. "He wasn't expecting a party."

I shrug as nonchalantly as possible and glance over my shoulder at the guys. "They're looking for work, too. They know their shit and can be an asset. Erjon will want to hear what they have to say."

Come on, asshole. Take the bait.

He nods toward two guys sitting on stools at the bar, and they hustle over and pat us down. A third man appears in the hallway and waves a metal detector over us.

We were right to assume there was no way to get weapons in with us. If we had tried, we'd already be dead.

Once we're cleared, the big guy leads us down a narrow, dark hallway. In all the times I was here all those years ago, I never made it back here. Saban preferred to operate out of the restaurant down the street. This place was for relaxing. Where he and his lackeys would come to unwind and indulge in booze and the girls.

I never quite understood why Aleksander moved his head-quarters here after Saban's death, though maybe it had some-thing to do with the fact that his brother died in that office.

The hall ends at a solid emergency door, and a handful of

doors line either side. We stop in front of a closed door on the left, and the goon knocks and pushes it open then waves us in.

I enter first.

Every single one of us would have preferred for Cutter to lead the way, but not in this game. I'm the one Erjon wants to see. I'm the one who will make or break this.

It's up to me to make this succeed.

My hands fist at my sides, stepping through the jamb. The small office would feel tight with just the four of us, but with the massive wooden desk Erjon sits behind and a goon on either wall to our sides, it's more like being crammed into a sardine can.

Sweat trickles down my back, and I move forward until only the few feet of the wooden desktop separates me from the man in charge.

His hard, dark eyes roam over each one of us and come to rest on me. One corner of his lips curls into a humorless half-smile. "Well, well, well. Elijah Swift. I never thought you'd have the balls to set foot in here again."

I wouldn't if it weren't for Eva.

I force a grin. "I'm ready to come back."

He barks out a laugh and drops his head back against the leather of the high-back chair he rules from. "Come back? What makes you think anyone here wants you anywhere near our business after what you did?"

Heat crawls over my skin.

What I did?

I shrug and glance around the room. "I'm not the same person I was ten years ago. I understand now."

One of his dark eyebrows rises. "You understand what?"

This will be the hardest lie I've ever told. "What this business requires. What it takes to survive and succeed." I swallow thickly. "Loyalty to who matters. Nothing holding you back or affecting your decisions. No liabilities."

A slow grin spreads across his face. "I'm pleased your time in prison has taught you such a valuable lesson, Elijah. But what could you possibly have to offer me?"

I wave a hand over Rion, Warwick, and Cutter. As planned, they've remained silent to leave me to do all the talking. "An experienced crew who also knows what it takes. People willing to do the dirty work."

His gaze travels over them again. "What is it you think I need help with?"

This is where things could get dicey.

I can't give away all that we know, but I need to make it clear to Erjon how valuable we can be to his organization if we have any hope of learning something that will help us dismantle the pipeline they've created to take and bring in these women.

I press my palms flat on the desk and lean forward. "We've heard you've branched out since you took over. To new endeavors that may require a skillset we possess."

He rubs his finger over his lips. "What skillset is that?"

"Smuggling. Transportation. Knowledge of the water."

Those already dark eyes deepen to an almost black. "What is it you think you know, Mr. Swift?"

"That the boat on the news, the one found in the lake with special *cargo*, is yours. Your shipment never made it here, and that means you're in desperate need of replenishment. We can assist you in this endeavor."

He rocks back in his chair and steeples his hands over his mouth. "Well, Mr. Swift, you sure do have a lot of balls coming in here and suggesting I am involved in any such vile business."

I snort and shake my head. "Cut the crap, Erjon. We're experienced sailors with our own boats and connections to get in and out of the country without any prying eyes seeing what's being held in our cargo holds. Either you want our help or not."

If he's smart, Erjon will be wondering if we're the ones behind the hijacking and murder of his men on that ship and the one that made it to port. Which will mean he will order these men standing on either side of us to take us out without a second thought. But if he's *really* smart, he will recognize that anyone who could do *that* is a huge asset to his organization that he shouldn't be so quick to dismiss.

The only question is, does he have a cool enough head to make the rational, reasoned decision, or will he lash out and seek revenge?

A tiny grin pulls at his lips, and he leans forward in his chair toward me. "Are you the one fucking the whore missing from the ship, or is it one of these guys?" He waves his hand toward Cutter, Warwick, and Rion.

Motherfucker!

The anger toward the man responsible for all of this that's been simmering just below the surface for weeks finally boils over. I grab his arm and use it to leverage myself across the desk to wrap my hands around his throat.

"Shit!" Cutter moves as quick as lightning and strikes, taking out the guy to the right of the desk, and Warwick and Rion disable the man on the left.

I tighten my hold on Erjon, digging my thumbs against his windpipe. "You motherfucking piece of shit. Do you have any idea what you've done to those girls?"

He gasps and claws at my arms, but I only increase the pressure and force him to struggle for air. Nothing he's doing can hurt me. Not any more than anything I've already experienced.

"I will fucking kill you, you piece of shit disgrace for a human being. I will—"

The door opening behind me has me jerking my head around. Cutter and Rion raise the weapons they took from the goons at the man in the dark suit standing in the doorway.

He holds up his hands with a lop-sided grin. "Well, this is awkward." He takes a step into the room and motions for Cutter and Rion to lower their weapons. "Don't worry, boys, we're on the same side here."

Who the fuck is this guy?

Cutter keeps his weapon trained on the man, as does Rion. We aren't that stupid.

The man focuses on where my hands are still wrapped around Erjon's neck, and a low, dark chuckle slips from his lips. "Well, Erjon, it seems the tables have turned. It looks like I arrived at the right time to discuss my future in this organization."

Warwick nods at the man. "Who the fuck are you?"

If he's a member of Erjon's organization, then Cutter and Rion should be taking him out now. The element of surprise and ability to plan a targeted strike was lost the second I leaped across this desk and grabbed Erjon. I lost my fucking temper, and that means we lost any thought-out plan.

The only way we're getting out of here alive now is to shoot our way out. And whoever this man is, he's just one more obstacle.

He leans a hip against the edge of the desk and grins at all of us. "My name is Michael Syla." He glances at Erjon struggling for air. "Erjon's predecessor made me certain promises, ones that unfortunately died with him." One of his hands shifts over to unbutton his suit coat. "And I'm not one to sit by and watch someone else take what's mine. I've bided my time, waiting for the opportunity when Erjon would be vulnerable." A smirk spreads across his lips, and he chuckles with a wave around the room. "But I certainly didn't expect *this.*"

Where is this asshole going with this?

One of the goons on the floor stirs, and Cutter's boot connects with his head. "Stay down, motherfucker."

The only reason he hasn't already blown the two goons away is the unwanted attraction the gunshots would bring.

Erjon squirms in my hold, trying to wrench himself free, and I squeeze harder and focus on the suited man. "What the fuck are you getting at?"

Michael shrugs and reaches into his jacket.

Cutter steps forward and places the gun to his head. "I wouldn't do that if I were you."

"I'm just grabbing a smoke." He pulls open the jacket and slowly removes a pack of cigarettes from an interior pocket. He shakes out one and lights it, and Cutter takes a step back. "Boys, we're on the same side here. You want Erjon gone, and I want what's mine."

Warwick crosses his arms over his chest. "Which is what?"

Michael inhales from the cigarette and slowly blows out a ring of smoke. "That chair." He points to where Erjon sags over the desk then waves his arms. "This organization."

Rion snorts and shakes his head. "And what, we're just going to hand it over to you?"

This guy must be fucking insane.

He pushes off the desk and wanders around behind Erjon's chair. He rests his elbows on the back and stares down and the man whose life is literally in my hands. "Yes. You are. Because I can make guarantees."

War steps up next to me. "What kind of guarantees."

Michael inhales again and blows the smoke up toward the ceiling. "Whatever kind you need that ends with me sitting here and you all walking out of here happy."

Too good to be true.

No one walks into a room and gives a blanket statement like that. No one sane, at least.

I shake my head and twist Erjon's neck in my grip. He gurgles, but his resistance is waning. If I tighten the pressure for another minute, he'll be dead, and this will be all over. "I don't buy what you're selling."

Michael tilts his head back and laughs. "Let me explain something. I have no beef with you." He takes a drag. "My beef is with him." He waves his cigarette at Erjon. "And it looks like you're going to take care of my problem for me. It's only fair I owe you something. As long as it's reasonable, I have no reason not to offer you what you want."

Can it really be that easy?

We know nothing about this guy. Who he is. Where he came from. His ultimate game plan. We might be trading one monster for another.

I glance at Warwick, who looks to Rion and Cutter. They just shrug. This isn't exactly the show-down we were expecting, but it may work in our favor.

Michael leans back against the wall behind him and puffs at his cigarette. His gaze drifts to my hands around Erjon's neck. "What is *your* beef with Erjon?"

Warwick glances at me before answering. "We rescued a boat full of women he was trafficking. We want it to stop."

A grin splits Michael's face. "That's it?" He raises an eyebrow. "Done. That was never part of my business plan, and frankly, the whole thing is quite distasteful to me."

Again, too easy.

I shift my hold on Erjon, my hands starting to ache from applying the pressure on him this entire time. "And in return?"

He shrugs and points to me. "You finish what you've started and leave me to clean up the rest my own way."

Rion moves forward. "You really think we're going to let you step in here and take over when we don't have a fucking clue who you are?"

Michael chuckles and shakes his head. "Do you have a choice?"

Three men appear at the doorway with automatic rifles aimed at us.

Fuck.

There's only one way in and one way out, now blocked by a whole lot of firepower.

Michael waves toward them. "These men saw the writing

on the wall and decided to become part of my organization. I'd hate to see them have to leave bloodstains in my new office."

He's right. We don't have a choice right now. There's only one way we're leaving with our lives, and that's to cut a deal with him. If things change down the road, we can always remove him the way we planned to remove Erjon.

Warwick nods at Michael. "We'll take care of Erjon so his blood isn't on your hands, and you can say you stepped in to fill his shoes after his untimely death, and in exchange, you'll dismantle the trafficking lines. Deal?"

Michael smiles and extends his hand to War. "Deal." His gaze drifts over to Erjon. "Though I would have loved to take him out myself, this works in my favor."

And mine.

I tighten my hold and twist to ensure this ends quickly. Erjon sags, the fight totally gone by this point. All the rage I was never able to take out against Saban, all the anger that I've held inside of me for the past decade focuses through my hands until he's dead.

He may not have been directly responsible for what happened to Claire. He wasn't even part of the organization back then, but he's the kind of man willing to kidnap women and sell them as sex slaves. That's all I need to know to be confident that what I'm doing is righteous.

Now all that's left is to make sure Eva gets to her new life without me.

24

EVANGELINE

"Eva! Preacher!"

The panic in Everly's voice has both Milo and I jumping from the bed and racing out into the hallway. Preacher bursts out of his room behind me, and we move out into the warehouse until we can see Everly, where she stands at the top of the stairs, her eyes wide.

"Grace's water just broke."

"Oh, shit." Preacher glances toward the door to the warehouse. "The storm is still raging out there. Even if we called an ambulance, it might take it hours to get here, if it can at all. The roads haven't been plowed, and the one through the woods back here is even worse. And it's still coming down hard and heavy."

Everly peeks back toward the room. "What are we gonna do?"

I take a deep breath and push past Preacher toward the stairs. "We're going to do it here. I helped deliver two of my cousin's babies. I'm no expert, but we can do this."

Preacher nods. "I've never delivered a baby, but at least I

have medical training. Plus, maybe Rion will get here in time to help."

It certainly isn't ideal, but it's not like we have much choice. With this being Grace's first pregnancy, she could be in labor for hours or days. There's no way to tell. I learned that the hard way when Michelle went into labor and popped George out in less than two hours. We didn't even have time for the doctor to get to us.

I start up the stairs, leaving Preacher on the warehouse floor. Milo tries to follow me up, but Preacher scoops him from the floor.

He looks up at Everly. "I'll drop Milo in Cutter's room and go grab everything I think we'll need from Rion's room."

That's a good idea. Milo would be in the way, especially if things get dicey.

Everly waits for me at the top of the stairs. She grabs my wrist, keeping me from entering, and leans into me. "Can you really do this?"

"I can try." Probably not what she wanted to hear, but it's the truth. "Women have been delivering babies for thousands of years before there were hospitals and many still deliver at home even today. Let's just pray there aren't any complications."

Everly squeezes her eyes closed. "We got this." She takes a deep breath, opens her eyes, and turns toward the room. "Preacher won't let anything happen to her or the baby."

I follow her in. Everly's faith in Preacher and his abilities gives me some hope we'll make it through this.

Grace has her eyes and jaw clenched in pain. I know that look all too well. She's having another contraction.

I approach her and wait until she relaxes. "Grace?"

Her eyes open, and she sucks in several breaths.

"How far apart are your contractions?"

She shakes her head. "Shit. I don't know. Not long. I

thought they were just more Braxton Hicks. I've had them for so long, I just kind of just put them in the back of my mind. But these are different. And my water broke."

I drop on the edge of the bed. "It looks like we need to deliver the baby here."

Her eyes widen, and her gaze darts frantically from me to Everly. "What? Why?"

Everly stands on the opposite side of the bed and places a reassuring hand on Grace's shoulder. "The storm is too strong outside. An ambulance would never get here, and we can't risk not getting you to the hospital in time and having to deliver on the side of the road in the middle of the storm. This is the safest place."

Grace's brow furrows. "*Is* it safe? I'm not due for two weeks."

I grasp her hand. "That's still considered a full-term baby. If there are any issues, we'll deal with them. Preacher will be here, and hopefully, Rion and the guys return soon."

She nods and lets out a sigh.

I can't imagine Grace delivering this baby without War here. This isn't her world. It's his. And she got sucked into it. She had planned to do this with all the medical technology available to her and her boyfriend at her side, but instead, she's doing it with us and him stuck out in a storm.

Please, God, let him get here in time.

I grab Everly and drag her into the bathroom with me to wash our hands. When we step back out into the room, Grace is shaking.

Whether it's from fear or pain, either way, it's not good for her or the baby. We need to get her calmed down so her blood pressure doesn't skyrocket.

Heavy footsteps pound up the stairs, and Preacher enters, his arms piled high with supplies. He dumps it all on the desk behind us, and I grab a pair of gloves from the box he brought.

I need to know how much time we're looking at here. The

longer she's in labor, the more worried I'll get. "Grace, I need to check and see how dilated you are."

She nods slowly and shifts back against the headboard to a seated position with her legs spread and the comforter draped over her. Everly lifts it for me, and with Grace's help, I manage to remove her underwear.

Jesus. She's even further along than I anticipated.

"Grace," I squeeze her foot, "you're around five centimeters dilated. You're halfway there."

She must have been ignoring the contractions for a long time before her water broke and she realized she was in active labor.

"Shit..." Preacher leans back against the desk and rubs a hand over his face.

Everly shoots him a nasty glare.

She's right.

We don't need to upset Grace any more than she already is.

I pat her hand. "Everything's fine, Grace. Just keep breathing through the contractions."

She grimaces. "I don't suppose anyone knows how to insert an epidural?"

Preacher and I both laugh.

He grins at her. "Sorry, no. But I can look up what drugs are safe to give you. Unless you want a natural birth?"

She shakes her head, sending red hair flying around her face. "Give me the drugs. God knows I need them." She pauses for a few seconds to breathe through another contraction. "Did you call Warwick?"

Preacher glances between Everly and me. He runs a hand through his hair. "I don't think we should. It's not going to get him here any faster to know."

Grace looks ready to argue, but Everly sits on the bed next to her and takes her hand. Grace nods. "You're probably right. He's on his way back. He'll get here when he gets here."

Hopefully before his child enters this world.

Though my unease isn't just because I'm worrying about Warwick missing this. Rion is the best trained to handle any complications. If anything happens to Grace and we aren't able to help her, I won't be able to live with myself. She's been such a good friend to me and welcomed me with open arms.

I can't lose her. I won't.

Preacher and I organize all the supplies, and he starts an IV to keep her hydrated but also to make it easier to get her some pain meds.

He grabs my arm and pulls me to the side. "I'm scrolling through a few websites and reading up on the basics of delivering a baby." He glances over at Everly, who's holding Grace's hand and trying to help her breathe through each contraction.

The wind howls, rattling the warehouse. There doesn't seem to be any sign of the storm letting up. It continues to rage outside, and the timing for this could not be worse. The guys' return will be slowed, and we won't be able to get her out of here if there are complications.

It's yet another reminder how out of control and out of our hands things really are. If anything goes wrong, this could be catastrophic.

Don't think like that.

If the last few weeks have taught me anything, it's that something incredible can come from a situation that seems grim. I should have died on that boat. I was ready to let the darkness take me, but then a light in the form of a broody, tattooed, blond pirate stormed in and changed it all.

I force a smile and move over to check Grace again. This baby wants out. "You're eight centimeters. We'll start pushing when you hit ten."

She's progressing fast. There's a good chance Warwick won't make it back for this. At least we have Everly to coach her through it while Preacher and I handle the actual delivery.

Grace grabs my hand. True fear lies in her evergreen gaze. "Have you done this before?"

"I helped deliver two of my cousin's babies." But I had several other family members there who had done it before. I'm not going to mention that to her now. There's no reason to frighten her more. "Between Preacher and me, we'll make sure you and the baby get through this safely."

Everly chuckles and shakes her hand out. "What about me? I'll need an X-ray after this."

Grace smacks her on the arm. "Knock it off. Your pain is nothing compared to mine."

I laugh and return to double-check we have all the supplies I think we'll need. Once she's fully dilated, this is going to move fast.

Preacher continues to monitor her vital signs. "Don't worry, Grace. There's no reason to think things won't go smoothly."

She curses through her clenched teeth and the muscles in her neck strain. The contractions are coming hard and fast. She's close.

Come on, guys. Get here.

Even though I have no doubt we can do this on our own and that Everly will help her through it, Grace will be so much calmer if Warwick were here with her. And we need her calm.

Preacher's phone pings, and he pulls it from his pocket. "Perimeter alert." His head snaps up, and he grins. "They're back."

Oh, thank God.

Everly pushes to her feet. "I'll go get Warwick and Rion right away."

An animalistic scream wrenches from Grace's throat, and she clutches the sheets.

The guys will have heard that even if Everly wasn't going down for them.

They could not have arrived at a better time. I check her progress again and confirm that only a few minutes from now, she's going to be pushing this baby out, and there's no way to stop it.

Footsteps thunder up the stairs, and Warwick bursts into the room, his eyes wide. "Oh, my God, Grace. Are you all right?"

She scowls at him and points to her spread legs covered by the bedsheet. "Do I look like I'm okay?"

I can't blame her for snapping. She expected to be in a hospital with an epidural and the best of medical technology available. Instead, she's giving birth here and almost had to without Warwick beside her.

Warwick drops to the edge of the bed and takes Grace's hand. "I'm here now, babe."

Rion appears in the doorway, his broad shoulders filling the jamb. He takes in the scene and smacks his palms together with a grin. "Looks like I'm just in time."

Preacher claps him on the back. "You could say that. I was gonna have to do this without you."

"How close is she?"

I check Grace again. "She's ready to push."

"Shit, already?" Rion races to the bathroom to wash his hands and comes back out with an apologetic look for Grace. "Grace, I'm going to have to—"

She rolls her eyes and waves a hand. "Go down there. Yeah, yeah, yeah, I get it."

God, this must be so awkward for them.

But it has to be done. Embarrassment can't be a consideration when Grace and the baby's lives are in our hands.

I move to the side and take Grace's other hand so Rion can get in position. Now that Rion's here, Preacher can help him handle everything. Warwick stands next to the bed, his skin pale and eyes darting all over the room.

"Warwick," I motion for him to move back. "Get your arm behind her and help support when she pushes."

He nods and changes his position. Grace shifts back against him, and he leans forward to whisper something into her ear. She closes her eyes and breathes in deeply, nodding.

It's a touching moment, one that's tearing my heart in two directions.

This is what Elijah would have been doing had Claire survived. He would have held her through her labor, comforted her and supported her and taken their baby in his arms.

He would have cried. There's no doubt in my mind he would have. Because while he acts like he's all hard, it's life that's done that to him. It's what happened to Claire. He would have been a very different person. Not the shell he's become. Not the man who cried with blood on his hands. Not the man who can't let himself admit what's happening between us.

Grace needs me here, but he is somewhere down there, and I have no idea what kind of shape he's in or what happened at their meeting with Erjon.

All Preacher told us was they were on their way back safely. The last time I heard that, E came back in a daze and fell into an abyss I barely dragged him out of. If he had to do what I think he did tonight, it could break him again and undo any progress we've made.

But he'll have to wait.

Another contraction hits, and Rion positions himself.

He looks up at the to-be parents. "I need you to push on the next contraction, Grace, as hard as you can for as long as you can bear down."

She nods, and a few seconds later, she cries out and grits her teeth while she pushes.

"That's it. Great job, Grace." Rion peeks over at me. "He's right here. As long as she can keep this up, we should be all right."

I nod, and Grace sags back against Warwick. "You're doing great." I rub her leg. "Just a few more pushes."

She growls something under her breath and clutches at Warwick's arms around her. Animal sounds rip from her throat, and she bears down with all the energy left in her.

Rion reaches down. "He's crowning. Just a few more pushes. You can do it."

Grace sobs and shakes her head. "I can't. I can't do it anymore."

I grab her arm and squeeze. "Yes, you can! You have to."

War whispers something into her ear, and she nods against his chest.

Watching the two of them together tugs at the part of me so desperate to understand what's happening with E. Grace and War met under the absolute worst of circumstances, yet they're happy. They're starting their family. They're planning a future *together*.

Why can't I have that with E? Why can't he see it?

I blink against the sting of tears and try to concentrate on the final few pushes. Grace suffers through them with a strength I'm not so sure I could have under the circumstances.

A few more agonizing pushes and their son is out—kicking and wailing and strong, just like his father.

Preacher looks to Warwick. "You want to cut the cord?"

Warwick's arms stay wrapped around an exhausted Grace. He shakes his head and kisses her cheek. The new parents watch Preacher cut and clamp off the cord then lay him on the bed to examine him.

No matter how torn I am in this moment, I can't stop the happy tears and smile. "It sure sounds like he has healthy lungs."

I lean into Rion. "Is Grace okay?"

He nods while he handles the typical post-birth issues, and once he does another examination, he pulls off his gloves.

"There isn't much bleeding, I think she'll be fine. We just have to keep a close eye on her and take both of them to the hospital once the storm lets up."

"Is something wrong?" The panic in Grace's voice squeezes like a vise around my heart.

"No." Rion does his best to give her a reassuring smile. "There's nothing wrong. It's just a precaution, plus they need to fill out the birth certificate information."

"Okay." She lies back again, and Preacher finishes cleaning off the baby and hands him to her. She tugs down her shirt and places her son against her warm skin.

I motion toward the door, and Rion and Preacher both nod and follow me out onto the landing. "You really think she and the baby are okay?"

Rion nods. "He looks completely healthy, and her blood pressure is good. Not much bleeding."

Thank God.

I close my eyes and inhale a relieved breath. "This could have been really bad."

They both nod their agreement, and Rion watches me for a moment.

"What? What's that look for?"

He glances down the stairs toward the empty warehouse floor and leans into me. "You need to go talk to E."

"About what?"

A long sigh falls from his lips. "About all the things that he should be saying to you and he isn't. About what he did tonight."

"What did he do?"

Rion's lips press into a thin line, and he shakes his head. "Ask him. And don't let him walk away from you until you guys have the conversation you need to have."

He makes it sound so simple. But nothing has ever been

easy when it comes to Elijah. There are a lot of things I want to say, but none of it will change what's going to happen.

I slowly make my way down the stairs and down the hallway. The closed door of E's room calls to me, but I don't stop on my way past it. Instead, I beeline for the bathroom and close the door behind me.

It was only a short time ago I was in here with him, watching him lose touch with this world and swim in his own despair. But so much has changed since then.

I've changed.

And I've made a decision.

Rion is right.

Even if he doesn't want to discuss the obvious, I'm not going to let all these things hang like balls in the air, waiting for them to come crashing down. I can't leave with things unsaid between us.

I make my way back to his room and push open the door. Elijah stands at the window with the curtains pulled open, watching the storm outside. I nudge the door closed behind me. The loud click seems to echo around the room.

He knows he's no longer alone, but he doesn't flinch or turn back toward me. Visions of the way he melted down after their last mission, the way he basically went catatonic in my arms and lost connection with reality flash before my eyes.

But this isn't *that*.

This is something different.

He's struggling, but he hasn't fallen down that same hole he was in that night.

I work my way across the room to him and stand at his side. He doesn't move. I glance over at him, but his eyes remain locked on the scene outside the glass. "Grace and the baby are fine."

He doesn't respond, even though I know he's relieved.

There's only one thing left to say. I force out the words I would much rather swallow back down. "Is it over?"

Silence extends between us as the snow continues to fall outside. The wind whips it around, swirling it and battering it against the window.

We never had anything like this back home. It's so cold. So sterile. It makes me want to climb under the covers and never get out again. A shudder rolls through me, and I wrap my arms around myself and wait for his answer.

It's a simple question.

Really.

Is it over?

One that he should have an answer for. Yet, the man stands as frozen as the ground outside.

25

ELIJAH

"*Is it over?*"

Her question burns like a red-hot, iron stake driven through my heart.

Is what over? Our mission to destroy Erjon? My own self-loathing and hate? My lack of desire to be in a world where Claire doesn't exist? Whatever the hell this is with her?

I work her words over in my head, twisting and turning them until there's only one clear answer.

"It's over."

Two tiny words. Words I struggle to get up and out of my throat, yet when they're said, when they're finally hanging in the air between us, the weight of everything that's been pushing down on me from all sides for so damn long seems to lift.

She must've anticipated the answer because she doesn't move. She doesn't utter a word. She just stands next to me, watching the world give us a clean fucking slate.

The softly falling snow in front of me washes away all the blood off my hands. It freezes and lets the last remaining vestiges of guilt crumble and fall off me. The cold, crystal-clear world outside gives me a breath of fresh air to fill my lungs when I feel like I haven't taken a deep breath in over a decade.

So, yes. It's over.

For the first time, it finally feels like I might have a future again. Like there might be a way for me to go on living in a world without raking myself over the coals every second, every minute, of every hour, waiting to be taken to join them.

And it's all because of the sweet, wonderful girl standing next to me quietly watching the snow fall.

That's why I am going to let her go.

I'm going to save her from the stain I would inevitably leave on her heart, on her life, in her world. I'm going to save her from the harm I will cause. I'm going to save her from ever experiencing what I went through when I lost Claire and became that shell of a person. I'm going to give her the opportunity to move on while it's still possible before I work my way so deeply into her heart that every beat only happens because she allows it.

I'm going to let her go before I break her. Because the life I lead will bring her to that. At some point, it's inevitable. It's what Warwick and Preacher worry so much about every day. And look at what happened to Everly. She was drawn into a fight that wasn't hers because of her connection to us.

I won't let that happen to Eva.

No matter how painful it is for me.

I finally turn my head to look at her. Tears shimmer in her eyes, reflected in the moonlight off the white snow.

She turns her head slowly until her gaze meets mine. Her bottom lip trembles, and she tightens her arms around herself.

"It's over." She repeats my words.

Hearing them from her lips gives them a kind of finality mine didn't hold. Like closing a door, turning the lock, and tossing that key out into the middle of the water so no one will ever see it again.

She understands what I mean—on all fronts—and she isn't going to try to fight me on it. She isn't going to try to beg me to let her stay or to come with her. She isn't going to try to convince me I'm making a mistake. She knows it would be futile to argue.

That's the only reason I'm going to allow myself to touch her one last time. To taste her lips and feel her body pressed against mine.

If she didn't understand, I would turn and walk out that door without looking back rather than lead her on or hurt her further, but she does, and that means we both can be selfish one last time.

And there's something I've been dying to do to her. For her.

At least I'm going to tell myself it's for her, even when it's really for me so I can know what she really tastes like and live in that memory instead of the bad ones that have haunted me for so long.

I twist to fully face her, and she does the same. Only a few inches separate us, but it feels like it might as well be a mile. There are so many things unsaid, so many things that *can't* be said if I want to be able to let her walk away.

For now, this world can disappear. It needs to melt away into the snow falling outside and disappear under the cocoon of pristine white.

I close the distance between us and slide my arms around her waist to lift her. She wraps her legs around me and squeezes tightly, and I press my lips to her mouth in a savage, demanding kiss.

It's goodbye. That truth is evident to both of us without saying the words.

She moans into my mouth and rolls her hips, grinding against my hardening cock between us. I groan and walk her to the bed. She clings to me like a lifeline, like the anchor she once compared me to.

We're playing a dangerous game, yet neither of us is prepared to stop it.

I lower her and lay her across the comforter, then I kiss my way down her neck and across her collarbone and pull her shirt up and over her head. I let it fall to the floor, and she shifts up to reach back and unhook her bra.

My fingers brush the straps down her arms, and I pull them off and toss it on top of her shirt.

Christ, she's beautiful.

And after everything that's happened to her, that's happened between us, she still looks at me with such trust and innocence in her gaze.

She lifts her hips to let me drag off her pants, bringing her thong with them. Miles of glowing, flawless skin spread out in front of me.

My cock twitches, and Eva drops back down across the bed, her dark hair a halo around her against the pale comforter. She's like an angel sent to me at the absolute worst time. At the time I can't give her what a girl like her deserves. But I'll give her everything I can tonight.

Even if it destroys me in the process.

I was too pent-up, too explosive to give it to her our first night together, but tonight is all about her. About what we can never be. I drop between her legs, and her eyes widen slightly. She starts to close her knees, and I push her thighs open, wedging my wide shoulders between them to force her to keep them spread.

Her inexperience should have me running. A thousand things should have me running. But not tonight. Not when the world has put us here together, snowed into our own tiny piece of Heaven for a few hours before the sun comes back up and sheds light on the harsh reality of our situation.

She needs this just as much as I do. A memory to bring both of us through any dark times to come.

I press a kiss against her inner thigh, letting my lips linger against her sensitive, warm skin there.

Her legs quiver, and her hands fist in the sheets beneath her.

"Just relax, Eva."

She lets out a long, deep breath and sags back, and I shift forward and drop my head to the apex of her thighs. I kiss my way across her mound then drag my tongue through her wet heat.

Sweet fuck...

The taste of her arousal sends my head spinning. My cock aches, and I grind my hips against the mattress beneath me to relieve some of the tension building in my body.

I probe inside her with the tip of my tongue. She gasps and shifts back, trying to pull away from me, but I press my forearm across her hips, keeping her prone. She doesn't know how to take the pleasure I'm going to give her, but I'm not going to let her hide from it or escape it.

What she's experienced has earned her a moment of pure bliss. One I'm going to ensure she achieves.

I glide my tongue through her core again, savoring her moans in my ears and her flavor in my throat.

She tastes like possibility. Like promise. Like salvation.

This woman came into my life and completely turned it upside down. She mended wounds I long thought would bleed forever. Just by being who she is. Just by being here and not letting me get away with running from my own anger and agony.

I suck her clit between my lips and roll it over my tongue. She groans, and her hands find the top of my head. She pushes down, urging me for more without even realizing she's doing it. I slip one finger inside of her. Then two. She gasps and squeezes around them as I lick and suck and work her up into a quivering mass of need.

In all the years I've spent living in darkness, I've never wanted to see the light more. Eva hangs on the precipice of an atomic detonation, and I'm the one with the power to unleash it.

I curl my fingers into her G spot and thrust them in and out of her in time with my sucking and pulling on her clit. Her nails score the back of my neck, and she arches her hips in time to the tempo I've set.

Her legs start to shake, and the pressure of her hands at the back of my head builds. Her breath devolves into nothing more than pants as she nears her release.

My cock strains against my jeans, threatening to explode while I roll her clit over my tongue and lick back and forth. She reaches the peak and hangs there for a second before crashing violently over the edge. Her body bows up, and her hips roll, her pussy rippling and clenching around my fingers.

I hold her down and continue to drag out her release, letting wave after wave of pleasure course through her until she's finally pushing at my head.

"God...Elijah. Stop."

The pleasure is too much for her, and I pull back and let her drift down to Earth. She peers up at me from under impossibly long, thick, black lashes. I've never seen anything so beautiful in my entire life. I gave her that. And I'm going to ensure she has all the pleasure she can handle tonight.

I rise to my feet and pull off my shirt then shove my pants to the floor. Her hooded gaze follows my every move, and I take my hard cock in my hand and stroke it slowly. Her tongue darts out across her lips, and I step forward and place one knee on the bed.

She reaches out toward me, but I shift away and press her arm back to her side.

"Not tonight, Eva."

Not any night.

I lower myself over her and position my shaft at her wet core.

Tonight, I'm going to show her everything. Let her experience everything. Have one final night of selfishness before I let her go.

Her legs fall open for me, and I drag the head of my cock through her release and push into her gradually. She moans and arches her body, her neck straining and her eyes rolling back. I roll my hips to push into her all the way and slowly withdraw only to repeat the action just as languidly.

Last night felt rushed and hurried—almost frantic.

It wasn't the way her first time should've been. *This* is how it should have been. Slow and sweet and all about her. Even though giving her pleasure and watching her get off has me hard as fucking granite.

Her hips move to meet mine, but I maintain my slow, measured pace. Our hips grind into each other, the head of my cock dragging across her G-spot with every thrust and retreat.

The groans and mewls slipping from her lips rush through my ears, driving me forward as she gives herself over to me completely just as I am to her.

All the reasons this can never work don't exist in this moment. They can't. And for a split second, I let myself wonder...

What if this could be forever?

I grit my teeth and shake my head, bringing myself back to the here and now. I can't let myself think like that. I can't let myself dream. I had my chance at happiness, and I blew it. I don't get another one. But Eva has all the time in the world to find someone, to find *the* one.

So, while I do have this time with her, I'm going to make sure she's too busy feeling to think. I slide one hand between us and find her clit with my thumb.

I swirl it around and grind down with my hips. She gasps

and shifts slightly, adjusts our position, then regains the tempo. Her entire body vibrates, and warmth spreads through my limbs. I drop my head and capture her groan in my mouth, taking the invitation to slip my tongue between her lips and tangle with hers.

We're one beautiful being. Two halves of a whole designed to fit together and fill the gaping holes in each other's hearts, even if it's only for a brief moment in time.

She freezes and gasps, and her body jerks under me. I thrust into her again and again as tears trickle down my cheeks. My orgasm hits me like a bullet to the chest, and I come inside of her, releasing everything I have left to give her.

I won't be here when she wakes up in the morning. I can't be. I can't look into those eyes that hold so many questions. I can't see her bottom lip tremble as she climbs into the car with Everly to drive to Liz's. I can't find the words to tell her no when she asks to stay.

So, I won't be here.

This is it. Our final moment together.

I collapse on top of her and roll onto our sides, my cock still embedded inside of her. Her breasts crush against my chest, and I press a soft kiss to her lips.

She offers a tiny little moan and snuggles into my arm, burying her face over my thundering heart.

My tears flow sideways down onto the pillow, and I bite back a sob that threatens to climb up and out of my throat. I tighten my arms around her, getting her as close as possible for as long as I can physically handle it.

A few moments later, her breath evens out and she sighs.

I kiss her gently on the forehead and inhale her scent, trying to memorize it for those lonely times I'll need it in the future. "Goodbye, Evangeline. Thank you for everything."

My whispered words disappear into the air.

And take what was left of my heart with them.

26

EVANGELINE

I knew he'd be gone when I woke this morning. I knew it before he even turned to kiss me in front of the window last night. I knew it before he gave me the most incredible experience of my life. I knew it before he thought I was asleep and he cried and said goodbye. I knew it the entire time, yet I still let last night happen. I still let him take that last piece of my soul, knowing I'm leaving today and that he wouldn't even be here to say goodbye to me.

A huge part of me wants to write him a letter. Wants to put into words how I feel about this entire situation, how I feel about him. I want to explain it all.

But I *have*.

I *have* told him exactly what he's done for me, over and over again, and I *have* explained to him that this isn't just some emotional reaction to the situation.

What happened between Elijah and me is very real. Even with my lack of experience, I can say that, without a shadow of a doubt. This isn't lust. This isn't puppy love. This is a deep, emotional, soul-searing connection I'll never feel again in my lifetime.

It's why zipping up this suitcase and dropping the wheels to the ground feels like putting the final nail in the coffin.

Because he's not here. Because I'm going to walk out that door and climb into that car with Everly and Preacher and become someone else.

Someone who doesn't know Elijah Swift. Someone who *never* knew him.

I pause at the door and turn back to look at the room where I spent most of my time here. The place where I found who I'm going to be and worked through what happened to me. The place I found love in the arms of a man who can never admit it. The place I'm going to leave my heart.

My gaze pauses at the window where he kissed me last night and on the bookshelf that holds the album that broke E so completely and finally stops on the chessboard that has sat untouched for ten years.

He might've come a long way in the weeks that I've been here, but not far enough to take what's right in front of him. Tears sting my eyes, but I refuse to cry right now.

I'm about to start a new life. I should be excited. Happy. Thrilled. Maybe a little scared. But I shouldn't be sad. I won't be.

I force myself out into the hallway with my suitcase and pull the door closed behind me. Each step I take toward the warehouse feels both like a move toward my future and like running from my past. Maybe it's a little of both.

Voices hit me before I turn the corner and find everyone seated around the massive table. Well, everyone but Warwick and Grace.

And E.

Preacher and Everly climb to their feet and offer me tight smiles.

Preacher meets me halfway across the warehouse floor and takes the suitcase from me. "I'll just go put this in the car."

I give him a nod and blink away the burn in my eyes.

Valentina smiles at me from her place at the table. She hasn't always been here as much as Grace and Everly, but she still offered me a friendship I never would've expected from a woman like her. She's a badass and powerful, and exactly the type of person I wish I could be.

But instead, I'm the type of person who will let E lie to me.

Last night, I lied to myself when I thought I would be okay today.

Everly makes her way over to me and smiles. "Ready to go?"

My gaze drifts toward the kitchen. The one place he probably spends as much time in as in his room

A small, soft hand lands on my shoulder. Everly's eyes swim with sympathy. "He's not here. He left early this morning before anyone else was up, and nobody's heard from him."

I swallow through the emotion, choking my throat and nod. "It's probably for the best. It would've been too hard to say goodbye."

She gives my arm a squeeze, and Valentina approaches.

"You know to call us if you need anything, right?"

I nod and swipe away the tears running down my cheeks. So much for keeping them at bay. Valentina pulls back from me and mutters something in Italian I can't understand.

Cutter snort-laughs behind her and shakes his head. "Wishful thinking, *principessa*."

She scowls at him over her shoulder and smacks him upside the head before she returns to the seat next to him. Only Valentina can get away with doing that to Cutter without ending up with a bullet in the center of the forehead.

He gives me a curt nod—frankly, more of a goodbye than I was expecting from him—and Rion pushes away his chair and approaches.

The big man scoops me up in his arms like I weigh nothing and gives me a massive bear hug. "You're gonna be fine, Eva."

"I know."

He lowers me to the floor. "Do you?" One of his dark eyebrows rises.

A genuine smile crosses my lips. "I do."

I might never get over what happened here, but I can get over what happened on that ship. And maybe one day, I can finally go home. If what E said is true and Cutter's friend can really make it safe there again, maybe there's a chance.

But my heart won't be with me. It will be back here in this stark warehouse full of harsh, hard, and wonderful people.

I glance back and up the stairwell toward Warwick and Grace's room. "Are they back yet?"

The brief moment I saw them early this morning before they left for the hospital wasn't enough to thank them for everything they've done for me.

Rion shakes his head. "No, but Grace says to call her when you get there to let her know you're all right."

I nod and zip up my coat. It would have been nice to see them one last time, to say goodbye to them and the baby before I leave for good, but another storm is predicted in the next few days, and Everly and Preacher want to get to Liz before it hits the Midwest.

I can't wait around anymore for Grace and Warwick...or E. So, I take one last look around the warehouse that's been my refuge from the storm of my life for the last few weeks.

The boat they brought me here in bobs in the water on the far side dock and the people around the table who made my recovery possible all watch while Everly and I walk to the door.

She pushes it open, and a blast of cold air slams into me.

I shiver and pull up the hood on the parka the girls gave me. "This is brutal."

Everly laughs as we hustle to the SUV parked just outside the door. Preacher sits in the driver seat, engine running.

At least it will be warm in there.

I pull open the back door. "Do you ever get used to this cold?"

She tugs open her door and shakes her head. "I've lived in it my whole life, and I'm still not used to it."

A sardonic laugh bubbles from my lips, and I shake my head and climb into the warmth. "That's not very reassuring."

Her shoulders rise and fall. "Spring and summer are beautiful in the Midwest. You'll like it."

I'm not so sure about that.

We close our doors and buckle our seat belts. Through the trees, I can barely make out the sparkle of the sun off the lake. Water is what took me away from my home, but that water is what brought me here, so I can't say I hate it.

Preacher throws the SUV in drive, and we pull out down the long, narrow driveway through the woods.

The last time I came down this road with Everly on the way to her shop, I never thought about how difficult it would be to get out of here when there was snow. But it looks like someone plowed this morning. Probably one of the guys.

It's still slow-going, though. And every minute that ticks by is one I have to fight the urge to throw open my door and run back to the warehouse to wait for a man who doesn't want me there.

Thankfully, the road opens up ahead of us, and as soon as we turn onto that, it really means I'm gone. That *he's* gone from my life.

I squeeze my eyes shut against tears threatening to fall and take a deep breath. I'm not going to completely lose my shit in front of Everly and Preacher.

No. I won't.

"What the hell?" Preacher slams on the brakes, and I jerk forward against my seatbelt.

My eyes fly open. A red truck blocks the end of the road,

preventing us from turning out on the street. "What's going on?"

Everly leans back, and a smile tugs at the corner of her lips. "Why don't you get out and see?"

"Out there?" The wind still picks up the newly fallen snow and whips it fiercely around us. "I don't think so."

Preacher glances over at me. "Get out."

"What? Are they insane?" I lean forward to look out the front windshield, and my breath catches in my chest.

E stands at the hood of the truck, staring right back at me with hard eyes.

"Elijah!" I scramble to unbuckle my belt and throw open my door. Even the cold wind can't stop me from stepping out and closing the door.

Why is he here? Why did he stop us?

I'm not going to run to him only to have my heart broken again.

My boots crunch over the snow as I make my way toward him. He must be freezing in only jeans and a T-shirt—his tattoo-covered arms exposed to the elements—but he doesn't seem to notice.

His focus is trained on me, a tempest storming in his blue eyes.

I stop a few feet from him. "Did you come back to say goodbye?

He opens and closes his fists at his sides. His jaw clenches hard.

I raise an eyebrow and wait for his response. The wind kicks up, and snow stings the side of my face. "Look, Elijah if you—"

"No." He takes a single step toward me.

"No, what?"

"No," he shakes his head, "I didn't come to say goodbye."

"Then, what the hell do you want, Elijah?"

E throws up his hands. "The fuck if I know, Eva. That's the problem." He shoves his fingers through his hair. "I've spent ten years not letting myself want anything. But then... you came along. And you threw my world into total chaos. You made me want things I didn't think were possible anymore. You made me feel things I didn't think were possible anymore. You made my heart—that I thought was long ago dead and buried with Claire and the baby—beat again."

Tears trickle on my cheeks.

Is he saying what I think he's saying?

I can't afford to let myself hope for it. Not when another rejection will completely break me.

He takes another step toward me. "I went to see them this morning. I haven't had the balls to go there in all this time. I could never handle it. But I did it today. I was able to go and say goodbye. Because of you."

"What do you want, E?"

It's a simple question, and I'll repeat it as many times as it takes for him to answer it.

He closes the distance between us with three quick steps and captures my face between his palms, tilting my face up to him. "You, Eva. I just want you."

"For how long?"

A grin tugs at his lips. "For as long as you are crazy enough to want me."

"I'm not crazy." Maybe crazy about him, though.

"Yeah, you are." He brushes the tears from my cheeks with his thumbs. "You are if you want a man who's as broken and fucked up as me."

I laugh and shake my head. "I'm broken and fucked up too, E."

He grins and shakes his head. "No, you aren't. You're fucking perfect."

"If you really think that, you're in for a rude awakening when we get to know each other better."

In the grand scheme of life, we've only known each other for the blink of an eye. Not enough time to really know the ins and outs of each other.

He drops his forehead against mine. "I already know everything I need to know about you, Eva. I know all the things that matter. I know your heart, and I know mine can only beat as long as you're with me. *Here.*"

"Not in Kansas?"

"Not in fucking Kansas." He pulls away and presses a soft, reverent kiss against my lips. "Saving you saved me. Please stay."

Like there was any chance of me saying no.

"Okay." My agreement disappears on the wind as it swirls around us, creating a tornado of ice that blows away the remaining pain lingering between us.

He kisses me again, then he pulls back and smiles. "Now, let's go back inside. It's cold as fuck out here."

EPILOGUE

ELIJAH

ONE MONTH LATER

"Your move."

Evangeline leans forward to rest her elbows on her knees and worries her lip between her teeth. The low *V* of her dress exposes the swell of her breasts. Her laser-sharp focus centers on the chessboard, and she narrows her eyes.

I try to cover my smile with my hand. She's learning, but she's still making predictable moves I can see coming ten steps ahead. It almost isn't fair, but the only way she's going to get better is by making mistakes and having me exploit them.

Her hand hovers over her knight.

Don't do it, Eva.

Over the last few weeks, she's finally started to grasp some of the basic concepts and strategies. She shouldn't be making this mistake. She bites her lip and pulls her hand back.

Good girl.

Pride swells in my chest, and I lean forward. "What are you going to do, Eva?"

Her eyes flick up to meet mine, and a pink flush spreads

across her cheeks. It's the same one that appears every time I kiss her or touch her. I could drown in that damn blush.

"Stop looking at me like that." She crosses and uncrosses her exposed legs, the short hem of her dress riding up her thighs.

I raise an incredulous eyebrow. "Like what?"

She scowls. "Like you're undressing me with your eyes instead of focusing on the game."

My laugh booms around the room. I don't need to focus on the game. I could win with my eyes closed, but I like to let her pretend she's giving me a challenge.

"So what if I *am* undressing you with my eyes?"

She narrows her gaze on me. "Stop it. I want to finish this game, and then, we need to start dinner for everyone."

Dinner can wait.

Watching Eva get so worked up over the game—especially in that damn dress—has my cock aching.

The woman is sexy without even trying. It's a good thing she doesn't challenge me—at least where chess is concerned—because I can barely think about anything else than having her in my arms and tasting her on my lips while sitting across from her.

I nod toward the board but keep my eyes trained on her face, scrunched in concentration. "Make your move, then."

She licks her lips and moves her bishop. Her gaze flicks up to mine. "Your move."

I barely glance at the board before I move my rook.

A smile tugs at her lips, and a chuckle rises up her throat. "You really should pay more attention to the board, E."

She moves her queen. "Checkmate."

"Wait, what?" I jerk my eyes to the board.

Holy shit.

No one has beaten me in chess in so long, I forgot what it

feels like to see my king backed into a corner with nowhere to move.

She settles back in her chair and crosses her legs with a smug smile.

This was no fluke. She was *playing* me.

I reach over the table and grab her. She yelps as I drag her onto my lap.

"You cheated."

She laughs and shakes her head while her arms wrap around my neck. "Did not."

I press a kiss to her neck. "Did too. You wore this dress because you knew it showed off your cleavage and legs. You were intentionally distracting me."

"Hmm. Interesting accusation."

My lips find hers, and I suck her bottom lip between my teeth and nip. "Not an accusation. A fact." I rock my hips up, driving my hard cock against her. "And it worked. Well, done, love. I'm proud."

She grins at me and kisses me deeply before adjusting her position to straddle me. "You're not mad?"

"Hell no." I shake my head. "I'm proud. Just don't try that shit with anyone else." I grasp her ass in my hands and squeeze. "This is all mine."

"All yours." She kisses me again, and her nails score the back of my neck.

Heavy footsteps pound down the hall. "Whoa!" Preacher comes to a halt at the open door to our room. "Shit. Close the door when you're doing that."

"Get the fuck outta here. And close the door!"

He leans against the jamb. "Wish I could, brother, but we have a problem. Get out here."

Fucking eh.

I groan and drop my forehead against Eva's exposed breasts. "I'll be right back."

She sighs and slides from my lap. "Better be."

My cock aches, and I reach down and adjust it the best I can. Eva settles back into her chair and grins. I brush past her and follow Preacher out into the warehouse.

Warwick paces next to the table with Will held closely to his chest. Rion leans back in his chair, beer in hand, and Cutter and Valentina sit with their heads together, arguing about something while Milo stares up at them from her lap.

I see nothing emergent that couldn't wait 'til tomorrow. "What the hell is going on?" I drop into my chair with a huff. "I've got shit to do."

Rion chuckles and takes a swig of his beer. "I bet you do."

Preacher grasps the back of his chair and scowls at Rion. "Knock it off. We have bigger shit to deal with than you poking at E."

War freezes and glances down at the baby. "What's wrong?"

Things have been relatively quiet since Michael took over the Albanian operation. As promised, he stopped all operations relating to the trafficking ring, and he even managed to find the shipment still working its way here and diverted it somewhere he could unload the women and get them returned home. The MC seems to have let their disappearing members go without further investigation, or any they've done hasn't come anywhere near us, and the truce between Valentina and the Rose Cartel has held, too, so what else could possibly be going on to cause this level of concern from Preacher?

He sighs and scrubs a hand over his beard. "You know I've been monitoring the FBI files since the women were rescued from the *Wanderer*."

We've all been watching as the news coverage about the boat and women slowly tapered off to almost nothing. They were returned home without much fanfare, and the case seemed to have reached a dead-end.

War returns to pacing while rubbing his son's back. "Yeah, why do you look so worried?"

Valentina leans forward. "You're starting to freak me out, Preacher."

"We should be freaked out." His grip tightens around the back of the chair. "I just found a file. One that I've never seen before. One that was hidden in a very obscure file area. One very hard to find. One they wanted to keep hidden."

Cutter growls. "Yeah, and? Get to the point."

Rion tilts his beer at Cutter. "I'm with him. Let's get this show moving. I want to hit the bar tonight."

Preacher sighs and looks to each one of us before answering. "I couldn't get into it. The encryption is something I've never seen before. But I can see the file name. And we're fucked." He shakes his head. "It's labeled Great Lakes Pirates."

"Well, shit." Rion drains the bottle in his hand. "I'm going to need a few more of these."

I hope you enjoyed reading *Anchor Point*, the fourth book in The Inland Seas Series. The fifth and final book, *Dark Tide*, is available at all retailers.

RION

There is no black and white in this life.
The line between right and wrong blurs.
I'm constantly crossing it.
Saving a life is just as easy as taking one.
And I'm damn good at both.
Finding a woman who can survive in this world was
never on the radar.
But Gabriella pulls me from the bottom of a bottle
and touches me in

a way no one else can.
Too bad secrets and lies have a way of catching up
with everyone.

GABRIELLA

How did I end up here, slinging drinks at a dive bar
in the middle of nowhere?
The choices that brought me to this were
never even a glimmer of
possibility only a few years ago.
How things can change so fast...
And now, my path puts me on a collision course
with Orion Gates.
His bigger-than-life size and personality
should be a warning.
The profession he's chosen should be the
ultimate final straw.
But instead, I find myself unable to resist his pull.
A decision that could lead to the end of all of us.

Rion and Gabriella.
Lust and lies.
Betrayal and ruin.
This tide may drown everyone...

AVAILABLE NOW: books2read.com/DarkTide

Sign up for Gwyn's newsletter to stay up to date on releases and
other news: www.gwynmcnamee.com/newsletter

ABOUT THE AUTHOR

Gwyn McNamee is an attorney, writer, wife, and mother (to one human baby and two fur babies). Originally from the Midwest, Gwyn relocated to her husband's home town of Las Vegas in 2015 and is enjoying her respite from the cold and snow. Gwyn has been writing down her crazy stories and ideas for years and finally decided to share them with the world. She loves to write stories with a bit of suspense and action mingled with romance and heat.

When she isn't either writing or voraciously devouring any books she can get her hands on, Gwyn is busy adding to her tattoo collection, golfing, and stirring up trouble with her perfect mix of sweetness and sarcasm (usually while wearing heels).

Gwyn loves to hear from her readers.
Here is where you can find her:
Facebook:
https://www.facebook.com/AuthorGwynMcNamee/
Twitter:
https://twitter.com/GwynMcNamee
Instagram:
https://www.instagram.com/gwynmcnamee
Bookbub:
https://www.bookbub.com/authors/gwyn-mcnamee
FB Reader Group:

https://www.facebook.com/groups/1667380963540655/
Website:
https://www.gwynmcnamee.com

OTHER WORKS BY GWYN MCNAMEE

The Inland Seas Series (Romantic Suspense)

Squall Line (Book One)

WAR

Out on the water, I'm in control.

I don't make mistakes.

But the fiery redhead destroyed my plans and

left me no choice.

I had to take her.

Now I'm fighting for my life while battling my growing attraction for
my hostage.

Grace may have started my downfall, but she could also be my
salvation.

GRACE

The moment he stepped foot on my ship, I knew he was trouble.

He took me, and now, my life is in his hands.

But things aren't what they seem, and Warwick isn't

who he appears.

The man who holds me hostage is slowly working his way into my
heart even as greater dangers loom on the horizon.

War and Grace.

Dark and light.

Love and hate.

This storm may destroy them both...

Rogue Wave (Book Two)

CUTTER

Complete the mission.

It's what I was trained to do—no matter what.

But when things go to shit right in front of me, my objective gets compromised by a set of fathomless amber eyes.

This isn't a woman's world.

Yet, Valentina refuses to see how dangerous the course she's plotted really is.

How dangerous I am.

VALENTINA

The man who saved my life is just as lethal as the one trying to take it.

Maybe even more.

While he may have rescued me, in the end,

Cutter is my enemy.

The one intent on destroying everything I've striven for.

But the scars of his past draw me closer even though I know I should move away.

Cutter and Valentina.

Anger and desire.

Fight and surrender.

This wave may drag them both under...

AVAILABLE AT ALL RETAILERS:

books2read.com/RogueWave

Safe Harbor (Book Three)

PREACHER

When it comes to firewalls, no one gets

through my defenses.

For the past five years, protecting this band of f-ed up brothers has
been my mission.

But Everly pulls me from my cave and does the one thing no one else
ever has...

She makes me believe there's a life outside the world

on my screens.

Too bad actions have consequences, ones that threaten everything
and everyone around me.

Including the beautiful tattoo artist who has managed to etch herself
onto my heart.

EVERLY

The emotional upheaval of the last six months would be enough to
break anyone.

And I can already feel myself cracking.

A tall, sexy, tattooed bad boy is the last thing I need thrown into
the mix.

All I want is to keep my head down and pour my pain

into my art.

But Preacher walks into my life and offers me safety in a world where

I thought there was none.

Until our pasts finally catch up with us...

Preacher and Everly.

Fear and loss.

Hope and heartbreak.

This harbor may be their salvation.

AVAILABLE AT ALL RETAILERS:

books2read.com/SafeHarbor

Anchor Point (Book Four)

ELIJAH

Life outside the walls of my prison cell is far harder than the time I did inside.

There, I had my misery to keep me company.

Out here, I'm forced to face the reality of

everything I've lost.

Nothing can repair the gaping hole in my chest.

Yet, a broken woman wrapped in chains threatens to unravel the tangle of excuses I use to keep everyone

at arm's length.

But letting Evangeline into my world means exposing her to the real threat.

Me.

And all the terrible things that come along with that.

EVANGELINE

Taken.

Enslaved.

To be sold to the highest bidder.

The monsters who stole me away from my life

have no conscience.

I'm not so sure the man who rescues me is any different.

He's an ex-con and a pirate— not to be trusted.

But the dark veil of anguish that shrouds him can't hide the truth of
who he is at his core.

Elijah isn't the enemy.

He may be broken and tormented...

And exactly what I need.

Elijah and Evangeline.

Agony and regret.

Faith and acceptance.

This anchor may pull them both down...

AVAILABLE AT ALL RETAILERS:

books2read.com/AnchorPoint

Dark Tide (Book Five)

RION

There is no black and white in this life.

The line between right and wrong blurs.

I'm constantly crossing it.

Saving a life is just as easy as taking one.

And I'm damn good at both.

Finding a woman who can survive in this world was never on the radar.

But Gabriella pulls me from the bottom of a bottle and touches me in a way no one else can.

Too bad secrets and lies have a way of catching up with everyone.

GABRIELLA

How did I end up here, slinging drinks at a dive bar in the middle of nowhere?

The choices that brought me to this were never even a glimmer of possibility only a few years ago.

How things can change so fast...

And now, my path puts me on a collision course

with Orion Gates.

His bigger-than-life size and personality should

be a warning.

The profession he's chosen should be the ultimate

final straw.

But instead, I find myself unable to resist his pull.

A decision that could lead to the end of all of us.

Rion and Gabriella.

Lust and lies.

Betrayal and ruin.

This tide may drown everyone...

AVAILABLE AT ALL RETAILERS:

books2read.com/DarkTide

The Hawke Family Series

Savage Collision (The Hawke Family - Book One)

He's everything she didn't know she wanted. She's everything he thought he could never have.

The last thing I expect when I walk into The Hawkeye Club is to fall head over heels in lust. It's supposed to be a rescue mission. I have to get my baby sister off the pole, into some clothes, and out of the grasp of the pussy peddler who somehow manipulated her into stripping. But the moment I see Savage Hawke and verbally spar with him, my ability to remain rational flies out the window and my libido takes center stage. I've never wanted a relationship—my time is better spent focusing on taking down the scum running this city—but what I want and what I need are apparently two different things.

Danika Eriksson storms into my office in her high heels and on her high horse. Her holier-than-thou attitude and accusations should offend me, but instead, I can't get her out of my head or my heart. Her incomparable drive, take-no prisoners attitude, and blatant honesty captivate me and hold me prisoner. I should steer clear, but my self-preservation instinct is apparently dead—which is exactly what our relationship will be once she knows everything. It's only a matter of time.

The truth doesn't always set you free. Sometimes, it just royally screws you.

AVAILABLE AT ALL RETAILERS:

books2read.com/SavageCollision

Tortured Skye (The Hawke Family - Book Two)

She's always been off-limits. He's always just out of reach.

Falling in love with Gabe Anderson was as easy as breathing. Fighting my feelings for my brother's best friend was agonizingly hard. I never imagined giving in to my desire for him would cause such a destructive ripple effect. That kiss was my grasp at a lifeline— something, anything to hold me steady in my crumbling life. Now, I have to suffer with the fallout while trying to convince him it's all worth the consequences.

Guilt overwhelms me—over what I've done, the lives I've taken, and more than anything, over my feelings for Skye Hawke. Craving my best friend's little sister is insanely self-destructive. It never should have happened, but since the moment she kissed me, I haven't been able to get her out of my mind. If I take what I want, I risk losing everything. If I don't, I'll lose her and a piece of myself. The raging storm threatening to rain down on the city is nothing compared to the one that will come from my decision.

Love can be torture, but sometimes, love is the only thing that can save you.

Stone Sober (The Hawke Family - Book Three)

She's innocent and sweet. He's dark and depraved.

Stone Hawke is precisely the kind of man women are warned about— handsome, intelligent, arrogant, and intricately entangled with some dangerous people. I should stay away, but he manages to strip my soul bare with just a look and dominates my thoughts. Bad decisions are in my past. My life is (mostly) on track, even if it is no longer the one to medical school. I can't allow myself to cave to the fierce pull and ardent attraction I feel toward the youngest Hawke.

Nora Eriksson is off-limits, and not just because she's my brother's employee and sister-in-law. Despite the fact she's stripping at The Hawkeye Club, she has an innocent and pure heart. Normally, the only thing that appeals to me about innocence is the opportunity to taint it. But not when it comes to Nora. I can't expose her to the filth permeating my life. There are too many things I can't control, things completely out of my hands. She doesn't deserve any of it, but the power she holds over me is stronger than any addiction.

The hardest battles we fight are often with ourselves, but only through defeating our own demons can we find true peace.

AVAILABLE AT ALL RETAILERS:

books2read.com/StoneSober

Building Storm (The Hawke Family - Book Four)

She hasn't been living. He's looking for a way to forget it all.

My life went up in flames. All I'm left with is my daughter and ashes. The simple act of breathing is so excruciating, there are days I wish I could stop altogether. So I have no business being at the party, and I definitely shouldn't be in the arms of the handsome stranger. When his lips meet mine, he breathes life into me for the first time since the day the inferno disintegrated my world. But loving again isn't in the cards, and there are even greater dangers to face than trying to keep Landon McCabe out of my heart.

Running is my only option. I have to get away from Chicago and the betrayal that shattered my world. I need a new life-one without attachments. The vibrancy of New Orleans convinces me it's possible to start over. Yet in all the excitement of a new city, it's Storm Hawke's dark, sad beauty that draws me in. She isn't looking for love, and we both need a hot, sweaty release without feelings getting involved. But even the best laid plans fail, and life can leave you burned.

Love can build, and love can destroy. But in the end, love is what raises you from the ashes.

AVAILABLE AT ALL RETAILERS:

books2read.com/BuildingStorm

Tainted Saint (The Hawke Family - Book Five)

He's searching for absolution. She wants her happily ever after.

Solomon Clarke goes by Saint, though he's anything but. After lusting for him from afar, the masquerade party affords me the anonymity to pursue that attraction without worrying about the fall-out of hooking-up with the bouncer from the Hawkeye Club. From the second he lays his eyes and hands on me, I'm helpless to resist him. Even burying myself in a dangerous investigation can't erase the memory of our combustible connection and one night together. The only problem... he has no idea who I am.

Caroline Brooks thinks I don't see her watching me, the way her eyes rake over me with appreciation. But I've noticed, and the party is the perfect opportunity to unleash the desire I've kept reined in for so damn long. It also sets off a series of events no one sees coming. Events that leave those I love hurting because of my failures. While the guilt eats away at my soul, Caroline continues to weigh on my heart. That woman may be the death of me, but oh, what a way to go.

Life isn't always clean, and sometimes, it takes a saint to do the dirty work.

AVAILABLE AT ALL RETAILERS:

books2read.com/TaintedSaint

Steele Resolve (The Hawke Family - Book Six)

For one man, power is king. For the other, loyalty reigns.

Mob boss Luca "Steele" Abello isn't just dangerous—he's lethal. A master manipulator, liar, and user, no one should trust a word that comes out of his mouth. Yet, I can't get him out of my head. The time we spent together before I knew his true identity is seared into my brain. His touch. His voice. They haunt my every waking hour and occupy my dreams. So does my guilt. I'm literally sleeping with the enemy and betraying the only family I've ever had. When I come clean, it will be the end of me.

Byron Harris is a distraction I can't afford. I never should have let it go beyond that first night, but I couldn't stay away. Even when I learned who he was, when the *only* option was to end things, I kept going back, risking his life and mine to continue our indiscretion. The truth of what I am could get us both killed, but being with the man who's such an integral part of the Hawke family is even more terrifying. The only people I've ever cared about are on opposing sides, and I'm the rift that could end their friendship forever.

Love is a battlefield isn't just a saying. For some, it's a reality.

AVAILABLE AT ALL RETAILERS:

books2read.com/SteeleResolve

The Deadliest Sin Series (Dark Romance)

WRATH (Book One)

All I see is red.

Blood.

Pain.

Rage.

It consumes me.

The moment he took her, wrath invaded my soul.

I only have one purpose.

End him and take back what's mine.

Love isn't always clean, and wrath is the deadliest sin.

AVAILABLE AT ALL RETAILERS: books2read.com/DeadliestSin1

AFTER WRATH (Book Two)

They took something from me.

Something that can never be replaced.

They destroyed something.

Something that can never be repaired.

Only one thing can appease the burning rage in my soul.

Unleashing my wrath on those responsible.

The Dragon will rise.

Death will reign.

Because wrath is the deadliest sin.

AVAILABLE AT ALL RETAILERS: books2read.com/DeadliestSin2

SURVIVING WRATH (Book Three)

I fled into the night and didn't look back.

I grieved.

I loved.

Then he appears.

Dark.

Dangerous.

I never thought wrath would find me again.

But you can't run from it.

Not when wrath is the deadliest sin

AVAILABLE AT ALL RETAILERS: books2read.com/DeadliestSin3

The Slip Series (Romantic Comedy)

Dickslip (A Scandalous Slip Story #1)

One wardrobe malfunction. Two lives forever changed.

Playing in a star-studded charity basketball game should be fun, and it is, until I literally go balls out to show up my arch nemesis. When I dive for the basketball and my junk slips out of my gym shorts, I know my life and career are over. There's no way the network can keep my kids' show on the air after I've exposed myself to millions of people. I don't know how Andy, the new CEO, can go to bat for me with such passion. I also never anticipate how hot she looks in a pair of high heels.

Rafe's dickslip has made my new job even more stressful. It's hard enough being a woman in a man's world without dealing with sex organs being publicly displayed when someone is representing the company. But he's an asset to the network, not to mention hot as hell. I can barely keep my eyes off him or his crotch during our meetings. Defending him to the board puts my ass on the line as much as his, but it's worth it. So is risking my job to fulfill the fantasies I've had about him since he first set foot in my office.

Things may have started out bad, but... some accidents have happy endings.

Nipslip (A Scandalous Slip Story #2)

One nipple. A world of problems.

I own the runway. Until my nipple pops out of my dress during New York Fashion Week and it suddenly owns me. Being called a worthless gutter slut by a fuming designer is the least of my problems. My career is swirling around the toilet like the other models' lunches. Until smoking hot Tate Decker steps in with a crazy idea about how his magazine can maybe salvage my livelihood.

It's less than two feet in front of me. Perfect and perky and pink. And the woman it's attached to looks absolutely horrified. I need to help her, and not just because she's beautiful and has a perfect rack. Using my position in the industry to expose the volatile nature of our business puts my career in jeopardy in an attempt to save Riley's. I'm willing to risk that, but falling for her isn't part of the plan.

When love and tits are involved... Things can get slippery.

Beaver Blunder (A Scandalous Slip Story #3)

One brief mistake. A world of hurt.

No panties. No problem. At least until I slip on the wet floor and go heels over head in front of my colleagues and half the courthouse. Returning to consciousness can't be more awkward, until I find out who my sexy, argumentative, and bossy knight in shining armor really is. My career may not survive my beaver blunder, and my heart might not survive Owen Grant.

Madeline Ryan tumbles into my life on a wave of perfume and public embarrassment. She falls and exposes herself in front of me, and I find myself falling for her despite the fact she fights me every chance she gets. Being a woman in a good ol' boy profession demands a certain brashness, but it definitely has me thinking, maybe litigators shouldn't be lovers.

With stressful jobs and big attitudes, going commando has never been so freeing.

AVAILABLE AT ALL RETAILERS:

www.Books2read.com/BeaverBlunder